HOBSON HILLS SHORTS

VOLUME ONE

GRAY C.W.

❀ Created with Vellum

CONTENTS

PART I

A Beta's Love Song
A Hobson Hills Short
Hobson Hills Omegas: Book 2.5

AUTHOR'S NOTE

"The Beta's Love Song" is book 2.5 in the Hobson Hills Omegas series. The events in this short story occur after those in *Snow Kisses for my Omega*.

1

DAVID

"Tell me about yourself."

The young man sitting across the table neatly cut his steak. Romantic music played in the background, and candlelight flickered, creating shadows on the walls of the restaurant. All around the room, couples leaned in close to one another, whispering their secrets and sharing heated smiles.

David Bartley sighed. "Shawn, this is ridiculous. When Grey said he wanted to set me up on a blind date, I didn't think it would be with you. You're seventeen."

His friend had recently married into the Wilson family, and somehow, Grey had developed their nosy stubbornness.

Shawn Wilson grinned, showing off that charming Wilson smile, and David had to remind himself not to fall for it. Shawn was Grey's new brother-in-law, so nosy stubbornness was in his genes too.

"His intentions are good. He wanted to start you off with a comfortable date with no expectations. Then Gramps and Grammy found out, and things spun a little out of control.

My whole family is on the hunt for your one true love," Shawn said.

"This," David said, gesturing between them. "Whatever it is, isn't the path to true love."

Shawn leaned forward. "Tomorrow night, New Year's Eve, you're going to a party with Ray. He says it will be a night you'll never forget. You're going to love it."

Ray was a great guy, but he was twenty-seven to David's forty-seven. He was also another *comfortable* date. David had talked to the man several times when he came to the house with Carter or Juan, the town's two handymen and David's good friends. Ray had even fixed David's computer when the on button had broken.

If anything was going to happen there, as unlikely as it was, it would have already.

"So, again, tell me about yourself," Shawn said, chin propped on a fist. He tilted his head and grinned again. Damn it.

"What do you want to know?" David asked, giving in.

"You were a pilot, right?"

"That's right, sweet cheeks," David said. "I joined the military when I was a year older than you. I eventually completed flight school when I was twenty-six and flew plenty of missions."

Shawn's eyes widened. "That's so cool," he said. "Where are some places you went?"

"I've been all over Europe, Asia, Africa, and the Middle East. I guess my favorite was Istanbul. The Grand Bazaar was magnificent."

"Why did you leave the military? It sounds awesome."

David rolled his eyes. The military was so *not* awesome. There had been aspects of it that were great, but the overall experience left a lot to be desired. Still, he had helped quite a few people, so maybe he shouldn't be so critical.

"I did my twenty years and needed a change."

"What did you do after?"

"Commercial flying." David made a face and took a drink of his wine. "It was horrible. The company I flew for was very concerned with appearance. I couldn't wear what I wanted. I couldn't say what I wanted. I couldn't do anything I really wanted. That was the whole reason I left the military. I was an officer and making good money, but I wanted freedom."

"That sucks," Shawn said, wrinkling his nose. "Is that why you retired all together? You're old but not that old, right?"

David gave the boy a wry look. "Thank you so much for that comment." He laughed at Shawn's blush. "I make enough to live on from my pension, and I saved like crazy my whole life. My home here is the first house I've ever owned."

"I'm glad you bought it. The old family that lived there were jerks. They had a son my age that would follow all the omegas around at school and say nasty things to them. His parents just laughed it off when someone complained."

"Well, the house was definitely a fixer-upper." His big Victorian had a lot of potential, with good bones and plenty of space, but David was relieved that Carter and Juan always made time for him whenever he needed them. The handymen were both sweethearts and lifesavers.

"It looks better now than it ever did," Shawn said. He polished off the steak in front of him. "Do you want desert? Papa says they have really good cheesecake here."

"If you'll share one with me," he said. "I can't finish it on my own. This salmon was too good." David groaned, his belly full. At least, he hadn't had to watch what he ate on this date.

The waitress came over, and Shawn ordered a piece of the cheesecake.

"So, how was your fall semester and when does your Christmas break end?" David asked.

"We go back the tenth," Shawn said. "This year's been fine so far." He leaned forward, a shy look on his face. "Can I tell you a secret?"

"Of course," David said, leaning forward.

"There's this girl," Shawn said.

"All the best stories start this way," David said excitedly, clapping his hands. "Well that or *there's this omega*."

"Her name is Rebecca. She's so damn smart," Shawn said. "She's going to be valedictorian, and she's going to try to go to MIT for computer engineering."

"Impressive, but what's she like?"

"She's really nerdy. She kind of reminds me of Grey and Elijah. She likes comic books and sci-fi, and she's super smart. She's funny, but she doesn't mean to be." Shawn smiled tenderly. "She's really nice and is always the first one to step up when someone else needs help."

"Okay, sweetheart, I see it now," David said, on the verge of collapsing from the cuteness. "Are you two dating?"

"I want to, but what do I have to offer her?"

"You're in high school. Offer her a date. Take her somewhere fun. You don't have to marry her."

"What about the future? If I start dating her now and we fall in love, then she goes off to MIT, and I get left behind, what will I do?"

"Move to Cambridge?"

"I love it here, though." His shoulders slumped.

"Again, Shawn, you aren't marrying the girl. I love that

you're thinking about the future, but sometimes, you have to live in the moment. You have a chance to make some good memories right now. Don't miss it, because you don't know what the future holds. No one does, especially a teenager."

"Maybe you're right," he said finally. "She may not even want to go out with me. There have been... incidents."

"Incidents?"

"I hit her in the head with a basketball during gym. That's when I first noticed I *liked* her."

"Ouch."

"Then, I tried to talk to her at lunch and dumped my tray on her," Shawn said.

David covered his mouth, trying not to laugh. The poor boy looked mortified.

"Yesterday, she was talking to Mike; he's the guy everyone knows she has a crush on."

"Oh no," David said.

"I may have accidently bumped into him and suggested she had a boyfriend."

"Shawn!"

"I know, I know. It was a shit thing to do."

"You have to talk to her, Shawn. Now."

"What if she doesn't want to go out with me?"

"You won't know until you ask, sweetie pie. If she doesn't, then that's her decision, and you have to respect it."

Their cheesecake arrived, and they quickly polished it off.

"Happy so far?" Shawn asked, laughing at David rubbing his full belly.

"That was so good. I needed a nice, relaxing night. Thanks, Shawn."

"The date's not over yet," he said, standing and holding his hand out for David. "We're going ice skating."

"Oh my," David said. "I haven't been ice skating since I was a kid."

"I'll help, Mr. Bartley," Shawn said, pulling him from his chair. "Don't worry."

They walked to Shawn's truck.

"You really don't mind spending a Friday night with an old man?"

"You aren't old, Mr. Bartley," Shawn said. "To be honest, I volunteered for this date. I really needed a practice date with no expectations too."

Shawn held his door open for him, and David slid in, shaking his head. This teenager had been the most considerate date he'd had in a year.

"So, how did Cadbury's first day home go?"

"He's happy and adorable," David said, smiling at the thought of his sweet baby Angora rabbit. "He's just a little ball of grey and white fluff. I love him so much."

Shawn laughed. "Grey did good with his Christmas presents. I don't think anyone was looking forward to getting rabbits for Christmas. Then, once each of you held them, oh god, you all fell in love, one by one."

They pulled up to the lighted, frozen pond behind Farm Fresh. During the winter, the Wilsons allowed access to their pond every Friday and Saturday night, and at eight, it was hopping.

It looked like Barry and his husband, Jamie, had Friday night duty. The two men walked through the crowd, holding hands and making sure no one died.

Zoe's bakery had a stand up and running, offering hot cocoa and baked goods. David wondered why he hadn't come here before.

"Hot cocoa first," Shawn said, getting two pairs of skates from behind his seat.

"After that cheesecake? You sure know how to treat a date," David said, laughing at Shawn's blush.

Shawn paid for their cocoas, and the two sipped and people watched.

Shawn shot him a look. "So, I overheard Carter and Juan talking at Christmas dinner."

"Hear any good gossip?" David asked distractedly.

He noticed a girl peeking from behind a tree. She glared at Shawn, then slipped onto the ice, skating away at a furious pace.

"Carter said they finished your nursery, but he wanted to talk to Harper about making you a homemade cradle for the baby."

David turned to face Shawn, full of panic. "Fuck."

Shawn looked smug. "I didn't tell anyone, so don't worry. What's that all about though? You're a beta, like me, so you can't get pregnant, and I know you don't like women that way."

David ignored him and crossed his legs, admiring his thick, wool leggings and perfect, high-heeled boots. His legs looked good. He spread his hand on his knee, admiring his nails. His favorite red polish looked perfect against his dark skin.

"Mr. Bartley?"

"Oh, fine," he said, huffing, and turned toward Shawn. "It's story time, darling. So, I've always wanted kids. You're used to having all that family, but I don't have anyone. My grandparents died before I was born, and I'm not close to my parents or siblings. I've dated and dated and dated, but I'm tired of waiting. I'm forty-seven. If I don't start a family now, I'm afraid I never will. Plan A was to find Mr. Right, get married, then adopt some babies. That hasn't happened, so it's on to Plan B."

"I get it, Mr. Bartley," he said. "It's why everyone is set on you finding someone. We want you to have what we do. Are you adopting?"

"I hired a surrogate from out of state," he said. "She's gone through the process with two other couples, and this will be her last time. She's about ready to start her own family."

Shawn grinned. "That's awesome. Is she pregnant?"

"Yes. She's three months along and is having the first ultrasound tomorrow."

"Do you get to go? Can they tell the gender yet?" Shawn looked so damn excited.

It made David happy to talk to someone about it. He'd been holding in his joy for so long.

"She prefers no contact, but she always sends copies of everything the doctor gives her. I want to respect her privacy, so I won't go to Connecticut until right before the baby is born. Now, from what I know, this first ultrasound won't tell us the gender, but it won't be much longer."

"Oh my god, this is so awesome. I take it only Carter and Juan know. Otherwise, the whole Wilson clan would be all over it."

"Yes, so let's keep it quiet, okay?"

"You got it. Now, are you ready to skate?"

"I don't know. There's a girl out there staring daggers at you. I'm afraid she'll skate over me to get to you."

Shawn followed his gaze, then hunched his shoulders, trying to hide behind David. "That's Rebecca. Isn't she beautiful?"

He peeked around David's shoulder.

The girl was pretty, in a nerdy kind of way. She didn't look happy to see Shawn though.

"I think you need to get out there and talk to her," David said.

"You're right. I'm going to do it." Shawn hurriedly pulled on his skates. "I'll be right back, alright?"

"You got it, sweet cheeks."

David watched as Shawn expertly skated around the other people on the pond, quickly catching up to Rebecca. The girl glared and tried to skate away, but Shawn grabbed her hand, trying to stop her. They both toppled over in a pile.

Luckily, Shawn landed on the bottom.

Rebecca tried to stand up, long limbs waving in the air. David could hear her yells from his seat on the bench.

Straddling Shawn, she suddenly stopped yelling and stared down at the young man in surprise. He talked fast, eyes earnest, and David hoped it was good.

"Why is your date being manhandled by some girl on the pond?" Elijah Wilson sat beside him.

David looked around and noticed the young omega's alpha and daughter skating.

Olive skated well, but Carter was wobbling. The little girl held his hand, doing her best to help. His friend may be the best handyman ever, but he couldn't skate for shit.

"Shawn is having girl problems," David said. "No one is supposed to know though."

"That's hard to miss," Elijah said with a laugh, watching the two teenagers talk, Rebecca still perched on Shawn's lap. He turned his attention to David, practically vibrating in his seat. "I overheard Carter talking to Juan at Christmas dinner."

"Fuck a duck. Did everyone overhear them?"

"Possibly," Elijah said. "We're a nosy bunch and knew they had a secret." The younger man wrapped an arm around David's shoulders. "I go to my first doctor's appointment tomorrow morning."

"My surrogate has one tomorrow too."

Elijah bounced happily. "Oh, we're going to have so much fun, David. Our kids will be the same age, and they'll both have Grey's son too. Little Rue will be less than a year older than them, so I know they're all going to be best friends."

"Are you stealing my date?" Shawn interrupted Elijah as he approached.

Rebecca and he held hands, both blushing with hearts in their eyes.

"Well, I think Ms. Rebecca here stole mine," David said. "It's only fair that I've moved on, Shawn."

"Our date was going so well too," Shawn said, shaking his head.

DAVID SHUT and locked the front door behind him, then bent over to unzip his boots. The night had been wonderful but not romantic. He wanted a partner. Someone to stand with him and love him. He wanted a specific strong beta with a big heart and a sweet smile. He knew exactly who he wanted, but he would never belong to David.

He padded into the living room and opened Cadbury's cage.

"Hey, little man," he said, cuddling the grey Angora bunny close. "Did you miss me? We'll have some time to play tomorrow before my next *date*. Blah."

He put the bunny back into his cage and shut it. His phone rang and he checked the screen.

"Greyson, my darling," David said. "What were you thinking with this date? Shawn is seventeen."

"It was a good first date, right?"

"I *have* dated before," David said. "I didn't need a practice date. It *was* a good one though. Shawn is just adorable."

"He is a sweetheart," Grey said. "We're going to find you someone special, David. I promise. You deserve the best. Now, at Christmas dinner, I overheard Carter and Juan talking about something."

"Oh, my god," David said, exasperated. "Yes, I'm having a baby. I hired a surrogate."

"What?! I heard Carter talking about adopting a hamster for Elijah! You're having a baby? Why didn't you tell me? When is it due? I need details, David. Right now!"

2

___

SAWYER

Sawyer Gregor could have cheered and danced a jig when the plane finally landed. California to Maine was a long flight, especially with three kids.

"Dad, do you think Mo is okay?" Harry looked worried. Mo was their border collie and currently slept in a large carrier with the baggage.

"Mo is all drugged up. He'll be fine," Sadie answered before he could. His eldest packed her headphones into her bag. "Daisy and Chunky are okay too. Don't worry, buddy."

"We'll see them all in just a bit, sweetheart," Sawyer told his youngest. "Get your bag ready." He looked behind them. "You ready, Ryder?"

Sawyer's twelve-year-old popped his head over the seat. "I'm good. Do you think Uncle David will remember us? I remember him."

"I know he will," Sawyer said.

He just hoped David let him in the door. The thought that he'd get to see his best friend again after five years made the horrible flight seem like nothing. He could already see David's dark eyes dancing with humor and that mouth of his grinning. His mouth had haunted Sawyer's dreams since the day they'd met.

"What's the wooing plan?" Sadie asked.

She held her arms out for the carrier with Daisy and Chunky. He handed it to her, then grabbed Sadie and Harry's bags. Ryder already has his strapped on. His omega son waited on them all, grinning and bouncing in the aisle.

"I guess that's up to David," Sawyer said. "I haven't spoken with him in five years. I don't know what he'll think about us."

"He'll love us, Dad," Harry said, green eyes full of innocent certainty. "We're great."

Sawyer laughed and grabbed his son in a hug. He tried to wiggle away, but Sawyer hugged him tightly. "We are great, son."

It was late when they finally rented the car and got on the road. Their three pets were situated in their carriers in the back of the Jeep with the baggage, and the kids snuggled together in the backseat. It was time for their weekly videocall with their mother.

"Hey, guys." Jill's voice came through the tablet. "How's it going?"

"Hi, Mom," Ryder said. "We're in Maine! We flew here, and Mo, Chunky, and Daisy are okay. We're going to the inn now."

"It's called Hobson Hills Inn, Mom," Harry added. "They have Wi-Fi and cable and they let pets stay for free."

"That sounds nice," Jill said, vaguely. "I have to go now, guys. Work needs me. Have a good time."

Well, that was a short call, Sawyer thought.

It seemed like they got shorter and shorter, but he shouldn't be surprised. Jill had never been one to spend time with the kids in person. Now that it was more complicated, she put in even less effort.

Sawyer also noticed that Sadie hadn't said a damn thing during the call. His eldest wasn't adjusting as well as the other two. She had already resented her mom's obsession with work. After the divorce and Jill's move to France, it was much worse.

"Dad, there's so much snow," Ryder said. "Do you think we'll be able to sled?"

"I want to make a snowman," Harry said. "Why didn't we get to have snow back at our old house?"

"Because California doesn't get snow," Sadie said. "This is really pretty though, isn't it? Even at night. You'll love it here, Harry."

Three hours later, they stopped for gas. They were only about thirty minutes from the inn, and the boys were out cold, so Sadie moved up front.

"Dad, I think you should buy a ring for Uncle David. You need to let him know you're serious, that you're committed to making it work."

"Why are you so worried about this, baby girl? You know your Uncle David will be happy to see you. He may not want to be with me, but he always loved you kids."

"I want you to be happy. The boys don't remember it, but you were so... I don't know... Light and happy when Uncle David was around. When he left, you changed, got quieter. It never affected us, so the boys didn't notice."

"I hope he wants me too, Sadie, but we'll have to wait and see."

"You want to marry him, right?"

He wanted David anyway he could get him. "It's been five years. It may be slow going."

"You didn't answer my question."

He gritted his teeth. He hated being so vulnerable in front of anyone, let alone his daughter. "Yes, I would love to marry him."

Even after five years of no contact. Even without knowing a damn thing about his new life. His dream was to have David beside him, not as a best friend, but as his husband, his partner.

"Are you sure you'll be okay if we move here? You won't be able to go to the academy anymore."

"Trust me," she said. "That'll make me the happiest person in the world. I hate only seeing you guys on the weekends and holidays. That was Mom's idea anyway. We'll get a house here soon, right?"

"We'll know more in the morning, after I talk with him."

"I think Ryder, Harry, and I should stay at the inn while you talk. I know Ryder's excited to see him, but you need time to woo him."

"What's with all the wooing?"

"I *may* have been reading romance novels back to back. I think it's soaking into my brain."

Sawyer laughed. God, he loved his kids. They pulled into the inn, and a man ran out to help them with their luggage.

The tall man smiled and held his hand out. "I'm Ray. We've talked on the phone."

"Yes," Sawyer said, happy to see the man who had given him the best Christmas present in the world. "You didn't have to meet us this late."

"Mr. Green goes to bed early, so I knew no one would be able to help with your bags. I got your keys already. Come on."

He picked up three of the suitcases and headed for the building.

"Is that Ray?" Harry grabbed his Star Wars BB-8 backpack and ran after him.

Sawyer shook his head. Harry had taken a liking to the private detective, stealing the phone to talk to him almost every time he called.

Sadie opened Mo's crate, and the Border Collie clumsily hopped down. His medicine packed a punch. Sawyer handed Chunky and Daisy's carrier to Ryder, and he rolled the sleepy cats into the inn. He grabbed the remaining bags and locked up the Jeep.

He met the rest of them in front of three doors on the ground floor. "I only reserved one room," he said, frowning.

"Oh, Mr. Green made it three rooms, since you'll be here just for tonight and tomorrow morning."

"What? We're here for two weeks."

"You'll either be staying with David or you'll be staying at this nice little rental house Gramps found. He didn't like the idea of you all crammed into a room for two weeks. Mr. Green already refunded the money for the other days."

"Gramps? Is that your grandpa, Ray?" Harry stared up at the man adoringly.

"He's kind of like my adopted grandpa. He's the head of the Wilson family. They're all over the place here. They're also the reason I hunted down your dad."

"I like them then," Harry said, nodding. It was done. He'd like the Wilson family forever now.

"You boys go in here," Ray said, pointing to the middle room. Ryder and Harry rolled the cats in with them. "Ms. Sadie, you have this room. It has a nice view of the woods behind the inn."

Sadie smiled and carried her bags inside, Mo at her heels.

"Sawyer, this is your room. Come on, let's talk."

"Is there something wrong?"

"I've heard some things since the last time we talked."

"Okay?" They entered the large room, and Sawyer promptly plopped in one of the chairs, exhausted. The last few days had been crazy.

"You love David, right?"

"More than anything. I wish I would have realized it before he left."

"You know he's always wanted kids."

"Yeah. He loves my three, and he'll be a good dad."

"He's having a baby."

"What?" Sawyer sat up straight. "David is in a relationship? I thought you said he was single, and that his friend, Grey, would keep it that way."

"He is single. He hired a surrogate," Ray said, watching him carefully.

Sawyer breathed a sigh of relief, slumping in his chair. "Fuck, man. You scared me."

"Did you hear me? He's having a baby. Are you alright with that?"

"Of course." David had wanted kids so much. "If things go the way I want them to, we'll raise the baby together, right alongside my three."

Ray grinned. "Glad to hear it. Now I won't have to chase you out of town." He stood. "I'll let you get some sleep. You'll go and see him in the morning. He's supposed to go with me to a New Year's Eve party, but, assuming you don't screw it up, that date is all yours." He headed toward the door but turned back. "Oh, yeah. There's a bakery right across the street. Zoe Wilson owns it and insists you send the kids over there for breakfast in the morning while you talk with David. She's good people."

"Thanks, Ray."

The man left, and Sawyer looked around his room, the quiet eerie.

He closed his eyes, thinking about his life. He'd spent sixteen years with a woman that he didn't especially like. He had three great kids, yes, but sixteen years with a workaholic who cared about her job more than her family was hard.

He'd been free of her for two years now but hadn't found what he'd been looking for until Ray called him Christmas morning. In the modern age, it shouldn't have taken this long to find one man.

After a restless night of sleep, Sawyer wrangled the kids and fed the pets.

"You're sure you three will be okay at the bakery?"

All three nodded.

"You know not to talk to strangers, and Sadie is in charge."

"Why does she always get to be in charge?" Ryder wrinkled his nose, trying to look displeased but only looking adorable.

"Because she's fifteen and you're twelve. You have my number, and I'll be back as soon as I can. Hopefully with David."

A young blond in an apron popped up behind him, scaring the shit out of him.

"Hi! You must be Sawyer Gregor. I'm Zoe Wilson."

"Hi," Harry said, waving. "Ray told us you were really nice. Are you going to have breakfast with us while Dad goes and woos Uncle David?"

"I sure am," she said, walking them to a table right next

to the front counter. Three plates of bacon, eggs, and sourdough toast sat on the table.

Ray sat eating his own plate of food.

Zoe bounced from foot to foot. "Here's your breakfast, kids. I hope you like scrambled eggs. Can they have sweets, Sawyer?"

"They can, but in moderation," he answered, blown away by her consideration.

"Perfect! I got this. Go get your man," she said, pointing to the door and handing him a carrier with two steaming cups of coffee.

"Good luck," Ray said, smiling when Harry sat beside him and started rambling.

Sawyer marched out the door and walked the two blocks to David's house.

The town of Hobson Hills was lovely, but it was in transition. Christmas was over and with it all the magic and wonder. Decorations were in the slow process of disappearing now that the New Year was about to begin, and the windows and doors looked bare.

Sawyer could sympathize. He was in transition himself.

David's house was a huge pale blue Victorian with white gingerbread trim. He noted the small balcony over the attached gazebo, the bay windows on the second floor, and the spacious wraparound porch.

The front yard was small, but he could see a white vinyl fence, hiding a backyard. It was a house meant for a family. His family.

He took a deep breath and walked up the steps. For a few moments, he stared at the wooden door. The glass panels revealed a blurred, warm looking inside. He closed his eyes and knocked.

3

DAVID

David looked at the ultrasound picture, tears streaming down his face.

"Do you mind, Mr. Bartley?" Susanna asked. His surrogate was a nice, no nonsense woman, so hearing the worry in her voice snapped him out of his daze.

"Of course not," he said, voice rough with tears. "Twins. I'm having twins."

"The doctor said everything looks great and that I'm perfectly healthy. I sent the report with the pictures. He does want me to come in more often for check-ups than I normally would. Is that alright?"

"Absolutely," he answered. "Thank you, Susanna. This is just so overwhelmingly perfect."

"I'll keep you updated, Mr. Bartley." She hung up, and David stared into space.

He was having twins. Oh, fuck a duck. He was having twins.

He dialed Carter. "Hi, David. How's it going?"

"I'm having twins."

"Yes!" Carter yelled. "Elijah, David is having twins too."

"Too? Elijah's having twins? Is there something in the water?"

"We found out this morning at his first big check-up. Oh, he wants the phone," Carter said.

"David," Elijah squealed. "I told you our kids were going to be besties. Now, with Rue, they'll be a group of five. They could be a band. We need to think of band names. What about the Apple Dumplings?"

David laughed, feeling his panic lessen. He might not be alone in this after all. "Weren't they a gang or something? You and your apples."

"I can't help it if they're the best fruit in the world," he said. "Oh, by the way, has anyone been by to see you this morning?"

"No. Why?" David looked down. He wasn't ready for company. He wore a moisturizing oatmeal mask and his silk pajamas.

He pulled on his long, silk kimono robe dotted with roses and butterflies. There. Now he was presentable.

"Nothing," Elijah said too quickly. "Oh no, look at the time. I have to go." He hung up, and David stared at the phone. That boy was a strange one.

David checked on Cadbury, slipping the little bunny into the chest pocket of his pajama top. The rabbit poked his head out, looking around, content with life.

David quickly watered his house plants and washed up his breakfast dishes, whispering to Cadbury all through his normal routine. He sipped his coffee and finally settled into his most comfortable chair to read the newest Roxanne Baxter novel.

Just as he opened the book, there was a knock at his door.

"Figures," he mumbled, setting his book down.

He stomped to the front door and pulled it open, staring in shock at the tall, broad-shouldered beta on his doorstep. His light brown hair was a little longer, and there were a few more lines on his face, but those damn green eyes were the same. Sawyer Gregor stood on his doorstep.

"David?" Sawyer took a step forward, eyes imploring.

"You can't be here," David said. "No. I can't see you, Sawyer."

He tried to shut the door, but Sawyer held it open.

"I get it," Sawyer said. "I didn't understand when you left, but I do now, David. Please let me in. Just give me five minutes."

David wavered.

"Please." Sawyer held up a drink carrier. "I have coffee."

He opened the door, letting his dream man in. His *married* dream man.

He grabbed one of the cups and led Sawyer to the living room, then curled up in his comfy chair, knees under his chin. Sawyer sat on his ottoman, facing David.

"What do you want, Sawyer? Is it the kids? Are they okay?"

"The kids are fine. They're at Zoe's bakery right now."

"They're with you? Why didn't you bring them by?" He missed them so much, especially Sadie and Ryder. Harry was so young when he left. He wondered if they remembered him.

He sipped the coffee, trying not to think of the past.

Sawyer smiled. "I knew you'd want to see them. I thought we could talk first." He looked puzzled for a minute. "Do you have a rabbit in your pocket?"

"Yes," David nodded. "This is Cadbury." He petted the bunny's head. "What's going on, Sawyer?"

"You loved me," Sawyer said, shocking David to his core.

"That's why you left. I was married, and we were just friends. You left so you could move on."

David was mortified and felt tears well in his eyes. "If you know that, then why are you here? To mock me?"

"No," Sawyer said, shaking his head. He leaned over and wiped at David's tears, coming away with oatmeal. "I didn't realize it at the time. I just knew my heart was broken. My best friend left me with no explanation, no goodbye."

"I'm sorry, but I had to. I watched you with your family for three years, Sawyer. I can't do that. I need someone of my own."

"I know that now," Sawyer said. "Right after you left, I started to realize what I'd lost. Jill and I had been having problems almost from the start of our marriage, but I never strayed. I never felt anything for someone else. Then you came into our lives, and I felt so damn much, David. I didn't know how to deal with it."

"I thought you and Jill were happy," David said in a small voice.

"Appearances aren't always reality," Sawyer said. "Remember how much you hated having to *appear* a certain way for the airline you worked for?"

"Blah," David said, wrinkling his nose. "I hated them." He shook himself. "Let me go wash my mask off and get dressed. We can finish talking then."

"Thank you," Sawyer said, looking relieved. "Can I hold Cadbury?"

David smiled shyly and handed the rabbit over. "His cage is in the corner if you get tired of him."

"As if I could get tired of this little fluff ball." Sawyer held him up, looking the rabbit over.

David slipped upstairs, breaths coming fast. Sawyer Gregor was in his home. Here. Right now.

He looked in his bathroom mirror and cringed. His hair was held back with a thick, hot pink cotton headband, and his face was covered in mush.

He cleaned up and applied light makeup, then ran into his bedroom, throwing on some skinny jeans and a big, comfy sweater. It fell down one shoulder, revealing smooth skin and sinewy muscle. Perfect.

He grabbed some socks and his boots, then focused on his hair. Lord it was a mess. Thirty minutes later, he opened his bedroom door, coming face to face with Sawyer.

"Your house is beautiful, David. I can't believe there's so much space. You even have a full attic." His eyes were hot, running up and down David's body. Cadbury sat in his sweater pocket, eyes moving between the two of them.

"Thanks," he said, nibbling his lip. "Did you see the nursery?"

"It's adorable. Ray told me you hired a surrogate. Is everything going well? Do you know the gender yet?"

"Ray told you?" David propped his hand on his hip and arched a brow. "What's going on here?"

Sawyer looked sheepish. "Well, Jill and I divorced a little over two years ago. We separated right after you left. I looked but couldn't find you. I even hired two private investigators, but nothing. Ray says they likely just took my money and didn't try. Anyway, Christmas night, Ray called me. He asked me some very pointed questions."

"What did he ask?" David led Sawyer to the seating nook at the end of the hall.

"After explaining that he knew where you were, he made me answer some questions before he handed over your information. He already knew a shitload about me. He knew I was an accountant, had sole custody of three kids, and was divorced. First, he asked why I'd gotten divorced. Then he asked if I was in a relationship. Then he asked if I loved you."

"What did you say?" David watched Sawyer, heart hoping despite his mental reminders to not reach too high.

"I told him the divorce was amicable. We just didn't want to be together anymore. Then I told him I wasn't in a relationship, because I was in love with you and had tried to find you for five fucking years."

"You love me? It's been five fucking years," David repeated, eyes wide, heart beating fast.

"It could have been fifty years, David, and I'd still love you. When you left, you took a part of me with you. I had the kids, and lord knows I love them, but I will never be happy without you. I just wish I would have realized it sooner."

"Sawyer," David said, completely overwhelmed. "I don't know what to say. I've wanted you for so long, and you're suddenly here."

"We have time. The kids and I are moving here. My clients know about the change of location, but I work from home, so it's not really a problem. Our things are already packed and on the way to the inn now. I need to figure out housing, but Ray said that some guy named Gramps had a rental."

"You're moving here? Already?"

"Of course. I can't woo you from California. Fuck, now *I'm* saying woo. I swear Sadie is getting in my head."

"You're going to woo me?" David grinned, crossing his legs and fluttering his eyes.

Sawyer leaned forward, gripping his chin. "I'm going to woo the fuck out of you."

He pressed his lips to David's, and everything disappeared but Sawyer's warm lips and delicious taste. The kiss deepened and before he knew it, David was in Sawyer's lap, straddling him. He pressed as close as he could, wrapping his arms around Sawyer's neck, savoring the feel of the man he loved.

His hard dick rubbed against Sawyer's, and he gasped, grinding down. Sawyer's hands gripped his ass, squeezing and pulling him down while he arched up.

"David," he said, groaning. "Fuck, you feel good."

He kissed him again, and David writhed against him, desperate. They ground together, then David was there, coming hard in his pants. He clutched Sawyer's head and moaned, stretching and twisting in pleasure. He felt Sawyer come, body curving up and fingers digging into his hips. They breathed hard, kisses softening and lingering.

"That was," Sawyer started, shaking his head. "That was beautiful, David."

He smiled smugly, hugging Sawyer to him. He felt a little ball of warmth and sat back, looking at Cadbury in horror. "What have we done?"

Sawyer looked down and snorted. "We traumatized your poor bunny."

"He's just a baby," David said, stroking the rabbit's little head.

"We won't do that with our human baby," Sawyer said, kissing David's neck.

"Babies," he said softly.

"Hmm." Sawyer bit his neck, intent on marking David.

"I'm having twins," David said.

Sawyer's head shot up, and he grinned. "Twins? That will make five kids. You *did* say you wanted a big family."

"True." David buried his face into Sawyer's neck.

"Do you have some pants I can wear? I need to get the

kids and talk to the man about the rental. You said you knew this Gramps guy, right?"

"Gramps is the best, but you don't need a rental. You'll stay with me," David said, standing. There was so much to do. "The kids can pick out their rooms when they get here. There are two downstairs and four free ones on this floor. If all else fails, the attic can be converted to living space."

He walked back to his room to dig around for some pants, and Sawyer followed him, looking around the huge space. "Will I stay in here with you or do I get a guest room?"

David threw a pair of sweats to Sawyer. "I want you here, but the guest room is probably the better choice until we know where we're going."

Sawyer held the pants up. They were black with brightly colored peonies covering them. He shrugged and smiled. "I know where I want us to go, but if you need convincing, I'm up to the challenge."

He gave David a kiss and left the room.

David sat on the bed, fingers pressed to his lips. His man was here, in his home. He had another chance. It was so scary though. His heart had completely broken when he left Sawyer and the kids before. Now that they would be more than best friends, the risk was even greater.

4

SAWYER

Sawyer held David's hand as they walked to Zoe's bakery. He couldn't keep the grin off his face. An older man approached them, eyes fastened on David. Sawyer didn't like the hunger and disdain he saw in the man's expression.

"Mr. Bartley," the man said. "How are you?"

"Roger," David said, his nose in the air. "So sorry, but I can't talk. My boyfriend and I have somewhere to be."

David pulled him along past the man.

"Who was that?"

"A man I dated," David answered, making a face. "In private, he's a completely different person. In public though, he's all about appearances and what others think about him. I should feel sorry for him and try to be more understanding, but he was actually ashamed to be seen in public with me."

"That fucking bastard," Sawyer said, trying to turn around and go after the man.

David laughed and tugged him toward the bakery.

"Come on, Sir Lancelot. I want to see the kids."

David swept into the bakery, looking absolutely beautiful, and Sawyer swore every man turned to admire him. Fuckers.

The kids sat at their table surrounded by people with gap-toothed smiles.

Did Lauren Hutton spawn a cult or something, Sawyer wondered.

Ray sat beside Harry, showing him something on his tablet. The crowd parted as David and Sawyer approached, and the kids saw David.

Ryder yelled and clamored over an older man in his sixties. "Sorry, Gramps," his son called back. "It's Uncle David." He launched himself at David, and David grabbed him and spun him around.

"Ry Ry," David said with a laugh. "You've gotten so big, sweetheart. I missed you. Oh my god, you're almost as tall as I am."

He peppered the boy's face with kisses and set him down.

"My turn, Uncle David," Harry said. "Do you remember me?"

"You were just a baby," David said, hugging Harry. "You're almost grown now. Are you married yet? When did you graduate college?"

Harry laughed. "I'm just eight, Uncle David."

"Oh, I'm sorry," David said. "You're just so big."

He gave Harry his kisses, holding the giggling boy tightly in place.

Sawyer laughed at them, shaking his head.

David looked around, eyes landing on a frozen Sadie. "Sadie? Are you going to forgive me?"

Sawyer frowned. Forgive him? For what? His daughter's lip trembled, her eyes wide with emotion.

She pushed out of the booth and ran to David, tears streaming down her face. "You won't leave again, right?" she asked. "You didn't say goodbye last time. I don't know what I did wrong, but I won't do it again. Just don't leave."

David buried his face in her hair, hugging the sobbing girl. "Baby girl, I'm so sorry. You did nothing wrong, absolutely nothing. I swear I won't leave you again. Even if your dad and I aren't together, I'm here. I promise."

Sawyer's heart hurt. He hadn't realized she had missed David so much.

She rubbed her face against his shoulder. "I know you loved Dad and us. Is that why you left? It hurt for us not to be yours?"

"That's it in a nutshell, baby girl. Do you forgive me? I should have kept in touch with you and the boys."

"It would have hurt you too much," she said. "I'm not mad at you. Just don't ever leave again, okay?"

"Never," he promised. "You and your rascally brothers are mine now."

"Dad is yours too," Harry added, worried eyes on his sister and David. "We have Chunky, Daisy, and Mo too."

"You still have Daisy? Remember when I gave her to you, Ryder?"

"She was my birthday present," he said, beaming.

The calico cat was a snooty little jerk, but she loved Ryder and Harry. She puked in Sawyer's shoes every chance she got though.

"Let's sit down, huh?" Sawyer pushed David and Sadie into the booth and pulled up some chairs. "Who are your new friends?"

"This is Gramps," Ryder said. "He said that if you said it was okay, he would take us sledding tomorrow. This is Zoe, but you know her. She gave us food. This is Elijah and

Carter. They're Uncle David's best friends, even though he doesn't know it, and this is Olive, their daughter. Then this is Grey and Abel. They're also Uncle David's friends and wanted him to date Ray. We told them that Uncle David belongs to you."

"Good," Sawyer nodded, glaring at Ray.

The man didn't even look guilty. He just grinned and shrugged.

"It's nice to meet you all," Sawyer said.

"Why are you *all* here?" David looked pointedly at each Wilson. He kept his arms around Sadie, hugging her, and Sawyer's daughter soaked it up.

Grey cooed at him, making a kissy face. "Because you're in love, David."

"David and Sawyer, sitting in a tree," Abel started.

"K. I. S. S. I. N. G," Elijah continued at the top of his lungs.

"You guys are so childish," Olive said with a look of disappointment. The young girl was really good at giving disappointed looks.

Sawyer laughed. These people really cared about David, and he absolutely loved it. He knew that moving the kids there was the right idea. He might be able to talk David into going back to California, but this was where he belonged. Sawyer had a hunch that this was where they all belonged.

"Well, even though we're childish, we would like to take you all ice skating," Elijah said, then stuck his tongue out at his daughter.

"I've never been ice skating. Can we go, Dad? Please?" Harry turned big, sweet eyes his way.

"We can, but we need to go get our pets and our stuff from the inn first," he said.

"Wonderful," Grey said. "We'll meet you at the pond. I

want to check on my honey bunches. Harry, Olive promised to show me how to skate, so she'll show you too."

"I will." The little girl nodded solemnly.

"Gramps and I will help you move your stuff," Ray said, getting up from the table. "Tell Harper we said hello, Grey."

"Will do," the omega said, heading for the door. "He can't wait to be off bedrest."

Sawyer gave David a questioning look, and he leaned in to whisper. "Harper is his husband. He was shot protecting Grey from a crazy co-worker. He's getting better, but the doctor has him on bedrest for another few days." He nudged Sawyer with his foot. "Move it, big guy. I can't wait for them to see the house."

"Is there room for us all? We can share if we got too," Harry said.

Gramps snorted. "That house is plenty big enough for you all."

His eyes sparkled as he watched David and Sadie lead the way outside. He looked back at Sawyer. "Plenty of room. Did he tell you he's having twins?"

"He did mention that *we* were having two babies," Sawyer said with a smug grin.

Gramps patted his shoulder and left with the rest. Sawyer turned back to Zoe. "What do I owe you? Thank you for keeping an eye on them and feeding them."

The blond smiled softly. "You don't owe me anything. David is family, even if he doesn't realize it all the time."

"Zoe," he said, frowning. "They probably ate a ton."

"Doesn't matter," she said, shaking her head. "Family is family. Take care of him, alright? He doesn't realize how loved he is."

She disappeared into the kitchen.

"Come on, Dad," Ryder said, grabbing Sawyer's arm and pulling him outside.

Harry was already in Gramps's truck, buckled in and waving goodbye. Ray walked with the rest of them to the inn, and they piled all their things into Gramps's truck and the rental.

A short trip later and David was directing him to the garage at the back of the house.

"I didn't even notice a garage this morning," Sawyer said, parking next to the small powder blue Subaru.

"It's an add-on," he said. "I'm glad the previous owners built it, but it's easy to miss, since it's at the back."

They unloaded the cars and went in through the mudroom.

"This is our new house?" Harry's eyes were big. "It's huge. Do you think it's haunted?" He ran past David and darted up the steps. Ryder followed at a more sedate pace, carrying Daisy.

Chunky walked slowly around the kitchen, surveying his new home. The large, grey, fat tabby sat on David's foot and looked up, giving a small meow.

"What do you want, Mr. Chunky?" David reached down and picked him up, groaning at his weight. "Do you want to meet Cadbury? You can't eat him, okay?"

"Who's Cadbury?" Sadie asked. She had stayed close to David since the bakery.

"He's the youngest resident of Casa de David," he said. "I'll show you."

Mo followed the two to the living room.

Sawyer left them to it and set out the food and water bowls and the first litter box. He had to put the cat bowls in the mudroom on top of a cabinet so Mo wouldn't eat it. The dog loved cat food.

He jogged up the stairs to check on the boys. They were in the nursery with Ray.

"Dad, is Uncle David having a baby?" Harry looked snarly. "Aren't we enough," he asked, stomping his foot.

"He hired a nice woman to have a baby for him, because he really wanted a family. He didn't know we were on the way, Harry," Sawyer said.

"Is he gonna get his money back, since he doesn't need it anymore?"

"Harry!" Ryder poked his younger brother's ear. "You can't refund a baby. We'll just have a little brother or sister."

Harry rubbed his ear, scowling. "I guess that's alright."

"You'll actually be having two little brothers or sisters," Sawyer said, wanting to get it out of the way. It would be better to let them complain now and not later in front of David.

"Is the lady having twins?" Ryder looked startled. "That's cool." Ryder turned to Harry. "Having a little brother or sister is fun, Harry. I love hanging out with you, but I didn't think I would when you were born. But look at us now. I didn't even try to sell you to the neighbors, and that was the original plan."

Sawyer covered his face and groaned, but Ray just laughed, patting his shoulder. "You've got good kids, Sawyer. These two will be good big brothers, just you wait and see."

"We will, Dad," Ryder said. "Remember when Daisy didn't like Chunky when we brought him home? Then she got used to him and now they love each other. We'll be like that." He darted into the hall. "Which room is mine?"

"You two pick quickly. We're going skating, remember?"

The boys ended up picking two rooms at the other end of the hall. There was a shared bathroom between them, so it was perfect. Both were sparsely furnished, but considering all their furniture was on the way from California, that was a good thing.

David stepped into Harry's new room.

"My room has a window seat, Uncle David. Look, look," Harry said, bouncing on the cushions.

"It's the perfect room for you. Look over here," David said. "There's a little hidey hole." He lifted up a small board in one of the corners. "You can hide all your secret things here."

"That's so cool," Ryder said, following Harry. He stopped and stared at David. "Do you have a rabbit in your purse?"

David had a small brown leather shoulder purse hooked across his chest. Cadbury rode in it, his little head poking out.

"This is Cadbury."

Harry and Ryder's eyes stayed glued to the rabbit, and the two boys sat on either side of David.

"He's so cute," Ryder said. "Can we hold him?"

"Sure. He already met Chunky, and he kept licking Cadbury, so Chunky will either try to eat him or raise him as his own."

"He'll raise him," Harry said confidently. "Chunky doesn't even like chasing mice. Daisy may try to eat him though. We'll watch out for him."

The boys passed the rabbit back and forth between them while Gramps rolled their bags to their rooms.

"Thanks, Gramps," Sawyer said, then blushed. "I'm so sorry. I never caught your name."

"Just call me Gramps, son. Everyone does. You'll get used to us after a while." He smiled, blue eyes kind. "Sadie picked the big room downstairs. Where do your things go?"

"The room next to David's," he said, wishing he could just say David's room. He reminded himself that six days ago he hadn't even known where David was. He hadn't even known they were moving.

"Don't worry, son," Gramps said, giving him a sympathetic look. "Look how far you've gotten. You and the kids are already moved in, and it's just been a day."

"Good point," Sawyer said, nodding. "I can't believe I've found him again."

"Come on, guys," Sadie yelled from downstairs. "I want to ice skate."

The boys ran past him, clomping down the stairs.

"Come on, big guy," David said, grabbing his hand and leaning up to kiss Sawyer's cheek. "Let's go have some fun."

LATER THAT NIGHT, Sawyer's family was dressed in their Sunday best, awaiting the New Year with the town of Hobson Hills. Most of the town gathered in the high school's gym, eating and dancing the night away.

He sat with David at a small table, holding hands and sipping champagne. His man looked damn fine in a nice, fitted suit.

"Look at them," David said, sniffling and pointing to two teenagers slow dancing together. "Last night, Shawn was on a faux date with me. Tonight, we're both with the people we really wanted."

"You went on a date with a teenager," Sawyer asked.

David shrugged, looking unconcerned.

"David," an older, gruff man said, approaching the table.

He pulled Sawyer's lover into a hug, and Sawyer gritted his teeth, reminding himself that he couldn't punch every man who hugged David.

"Jonathan, it's great to see you outside the store. You

work way too much." David pulled Sawyer to him. "This is my boyfriend, Sawyer."

Jonathan scowled. "Damn it. I didn't make my move in time."

Sawyer smirked and shrugged. "As my daughter says: sorry, not sorry."

David rolled his eyes and elbowed Sawyer. "Ignore him, Jonathan. You know you and I wouldn't have worked. Marty Swanson has his eye on you and would have stolen you from me. I would have been crushed." David sighed dramatically, hand on his brow. "Woe is me."

Jonathan and Sawyer shared a look.

"You'll have your hands full," Jonathan said, winking. "Good luck."

The man ran away, laughing, when David gasped, swatting at him.

Sawyer pulled David into a dance, swaying with him.

"I love you, David Bartley," he whispered, nuzzling his man's neck.

"I love you too, Sawyer Gregor," David told him, settling his head on Sawyer's shoulder.

From the corner of his eye, Sawyer watched Olive and Harry dance with some of her friends beneath the shiny disco ball. Harry looked like a maypole as the little girls danced around the older boy.

He heard Sadie's laughter. She sat with a gaggle of teenage girls. They talked and talked and talked. Sawyer had a feeling there would be sleepovers soon.

Ryder and another young Wilson, Hannah, sat at an empty table, making a list of goals for the upcoming year. Sawyer couldn't help but grin as he watched the two. They were both more organized than most adults.

David stopped dancing and gave him a sweet smile.

He pulled Sawyer into the hall as the countdown to midnight began. David's smile turned to pure seduction as he wrapped his arms around Sawyer.

Sawyer pulled him close and kissed him. He vaguely heard everyone yell at midnight, but his attention was elsewhere.

He had a feeling this would be the best year of his life.

DAVID

David slept late, Chunky curled in the bed with him. The house was still quiet when he got up, but the kids weren't used to being out so late, so he wasn't surprised they were still sleeping at eight in the morning.

He put on the coffee and put out food for Mo and the cats.

Sipping from his cup, he checked on Cadbury, taking the time to clean the cage and refresh the bunny's water and food. He left the rabbit to his own breakfast and grabbed his phone.

Locking himself in his bathroom, he dialed a number he hadn't called in a little over five years. It was probably way too late to call her, but he couldn't wait any longer.

"Hello? Who is this?" Jill's voice didn't sound sleepy, and he heard voices in the background, so some of his guilt eased.

"Jill," he said.

"David?" Her voice was pure shock. "It's been over five years, asshole. Where have you been?"

"In Maine," he said. "You know why I had to leave."

She sighed. "Hold on. Let me find somewhere private to talk." He heard the background noise fade. "Okay. God, David, I can't believe it's you. Wait, did you say Maine? The kids said something about Maine when I talked to them last night."

"They're here. He's here."

"Fuck. Finally," she said, groaning. "I can't believe you left like that."

"Jill," he said, frustrated. "Do you know how much it hurt to see him every day and know that he belonged to you?"

"Yeah. That had to suck," she said. "We just really missed you when you left. He's there now though. You giving him a chance?"

"Of course," he said. "Like I could say no. They're moving in with me."

"But? You wouldn't have called me if there wasn't something wrong."

"Is it really over between you two? He says you two were never happy, but it sure as hell looked like you were the perfect couple."

"We are beyond over," she said. "You know how my parents were. They wanted me married, with two point five kids. I did what they wanted for so long that it was actually a relief when I got pregnant with Sadie. Otherwise, I knew Sawyer and I wouldn't have married. He's a great guy, David, but the two of us just aren't good together."

David closed his eyes. He was ashamed, but he was so happy to hear they'd been having problems, even though it pissed him off.

"Damn it, Jill. What about your kids? He has full custody. How can you be so casual about losing them?"

"Listen," she said, voice full of emotion. "I haven't told a single person this, not even Sawyer, but you're going to be their new parent, so I want you to understand. I love them. I carried each of them in my body for nine months and have never regretted having them. They made Sawyer so fucking happy, and I wanted him to have that."

"He adores them," David said, nodding.

"Here's the thing though. I never wanted them. Never. I may be a selfish person, but I simply never wanted children. I can't even blame it on work. Career or no career, it didn't matter. I swear, it's not just an excuse to do what I want. I'm not mother material. I had them for Sawyer and my parents."

His heart hurt for the three kids sleeping in his house. He hurt for her too. "Jill, you *did* have them though. You have a responsibility."

"I know," she said quietly. "I call them every week. I send them birthday and Christmas presents, and Sawyer and I both contribute to their college funds. I know I could do more, but honestly, I think it hurts them more when I do. I tried with Sadie when she was little. I think that's why she hates me so much. She thinks I stopped loving her. The boys know I care, but they see me more like a distant aunt."

"I can't fathom it," he admitted. "I hear what you're saying, and I know every person is different, but I can't fathom not wanting to see them every day."

"That's why you're there with them, and I'm in France. I can't be what they need. You can. I've never met anyone with a bigger heart than you, David."

"You deserve happiness too, Jill," he said, shaking his head. She had an emotional responsibility to them too, damn it. He did know her parents though. They were pushy and controlling. It was so fucking complicated.

"I have my happiness," she said simply. "I am very satisfied with my life, even though I do feel guilty about the kids. I truly do think my distance is better for them than if I tried to be someone I'm not. I'm not completely selfish. Mostly, yes, but not completely. It's just that not everyone needs nor wants a family."

"Okay," he said with a sigh. "You and Sawyer are over. You don't mind that your kids are mine now, and you know that we're all living in Maine. I'll send you our new address, and you can reach me here. You're welcome here anytime too. If you ever want to come."

"I may take you up on that," she said. "My parents haven't spoken to me since the divorce."

"Well, we're here." He hoped Sawyer wouldn't mind him saying that.

"I missed you too, David," she said. "I thought Sawyer would die when you left. He became a shell of himself. I knew why you had to go, before he ever did, but I still missed you."

"I miss you too, Jill." Their call ended, and David felt a weight leave his shoulders. He hadn't realized he needed that conversation, that certainty.

He worked on getting dressed, Chunky sitting on the bathroom counter, watching him in fascination.

"Alright, Chunky," he said. "It's make up time. Should I go with a light and sweet look today or super seductive?"

"Meow."

"You're right. It *is* a Sunday morning." He went with light and sweet and dressed in a teal, silk Calvin Klein jumpsuit he'd found on sale at Macy's. The bright color contrasted well against his dark skin. He looked damn good.

"David?" Sadie's voice came through the door.

"Come in, sweetie."

She came in, yawning, dressed in her pajamas. She carried Cadbury in her hand, and Mo followed her. The dog jumped on his bed and rolled around. Weirdo.

"Last night was a lot of fun," she said. "I'm glad we're staying. When are you going to let Dad move in your room?"

"Soon," he said.

The teenager sprawled out next to Mo on his bed and set Cadbury carefully on a pillow.

David sat beside her. "I talked to your mom today."

"Why would you want to do that?" She rolled to her side and propped her head on her hand.

"I was her friend too," he reminded her. "I wanted to hear what happened from her. I needed to understand some things."

"Like why she's in France and we're here?"

David eyed her suspiciously. "Can you read minds?"

She snorted. "Yes. You and Dad had best keep your thoughts clean."

"I'm sorry for the things you'll see and hear, sweetie," he said, shaking his head.

She just laughed.

"Anyway, I did talk with your mom. She cleared some things up. You know she loves you, right?"

"Not like Dad and you do," Sadie said.

"I don't know what to say, Sadie," he said. "I have this crazy, selfish theory, but... Never mind."

"What's your crazy, selfish theory?" Her green eyes were sad.

"What if fate, kismet, or whatever made your dad meet Jill so that I could have you kids? Maybe I just screwed it up by leaving. I could have had all of you for five years now."

Sadie smiled, eyes softening. "That's not crazy. Mom will

never be a real mother, but you will be a great dad. Maybe you're right."

"Sadie? She said she tried with you. What does she mean? When I met you all, Jill was never home too often."

"When I was really little, I remember her singing me to sleep. We spent time together playing, and she was home more often. Then it just stopped. She just stopped trying."

"You know that's not your fault, right? She told me she wasn't meant to be a mother."

"I get it in here," she said, tapping her head. "I wouldn't want her to force herself to be someone she's not. I don't want that for anyone. It's just hard to understand it in my heart. That's why I like your crazy, selfish theory. I was just meant to be your daughter."

David pulled her up and into a hug. "That's the truth. You're too smart and beautiful to be anyone else's."

They both froze, sniffing the air.

"Is that bacon," Sadie asked.

"Someone is making breakfast," David said. His stomach growled, and Sadie laughed. "That was Mo, not me."

"Sure," she said, rolling her eyes. They heard feet running down the hall. "We had better hurry. The boys will eat it all."

"Wait. I need my shoes." He ran into his closet and picked a pair of black heels, putting them on as he ran for the door, Sadie in front of him with Cadbury.

Sawyer scrambled eggs at the stove. He ran appreciative eyes over David, but toast and bacon were piled in the middle of the small breakfast table, distracting David from his hot boyfriend.

The boys already sat in their seats, eying the bacon like starving wolves.

Sawyer served up the eggs and everyone dug in.

David watched Sadie stick her tongue out at Ryder when he teased her about her hair while Harry snuck a piece of bacon to Mo under the table.

Sawyer sat beside David, hand on his knee. In that moment, David knew that this was his family. This was his man. He hadn't been able to hold back with the kids, but he had with Sawyer. He was scared, and he still was.

He thought back to his conversation with Shawn. He had told the young man that he had the chance to make some good memories.

He didn't know what was in the future, but he knew these four people would be there. That was enough to take a chance.

"Have you already unpacked, Sawyer?"

"Yeah. I had some time before the party last night."

"That's unfortunate," he said, pouting.

Sawyer and the kids stared at him with hurt eyes and devastated expressions.

"You don't want us here?" Harry's lip trembled.

"What? Of course I want you here," David said, baffled.

"Then why is it bad that Dad unpacked?" Ryder sniffled.

"Oh, because he needs to move into my room. If he already unpacked, he'll have to pack again."

"We'll move him," Harry shouted happily. "It won't be hard. You'll see."

Sawyer grinned at him. "I'm moving into the big room, huh?"

"I'll make room for your things in my closet. Somehow. Are you sure you need all those clothes?"

"I can't run around naked."

"If he gets too, then we get too," Harry said.

"No," Sadie said. "God, please no."

"Fine," David said. "For Sadie's sake, you can keep your

clothes. As long as I get you, I can deal with less room in the closet. I guess."

"I feel so loved," Sawyer said.

"I really hope the twins are girls," Sadie said. "I think I'll need the reinforcements."

6

SAWYER

SIX MONTHS LATER

Sawyer and David pulled up to the house. It was so good to finally be home. Connecticut wasn't that far away, but he'd missed the kids.

Harry and Mo ran out the front door and straight to the car. Harry plastered his face to the back window to stare at the twins as Mo ran around the car barking.

Sawyer got out and stood beside him, peeking at the two newest additions.

"You're finally home," Ryder said, running for David. "I missed you."

David hugged him, watching Sawyer smugly. "You see who he missed the most, right?"

"Oh, I see how it is," Sawyer said with a smile. His kids fucking loved David and weren't shy about showing it.

"I missed you the most, Dad," Harry said, then mouthed *I love you more* to David.

"Why are the babies still in the car?" Sadie pushed Sawyer and Harry out of the way. "Where's Penelope? She's my only hope."

Sadie took the infant from her seat and cradled her

close. The little girl had her daddy's dark skin and hair. She wore white leggings and a yellow tutu. A little white headband stood out against her dark curls.

"You and I will take over the house, peanut," Sadie whispered to her little sister. "I love your tutu, and now I need a matching one."

David and Ryder took care of Penelope's omega twin, Phineas.

"It's okay, Finn. We'll protect you from the girls," Harry said, running around the car with Mo.

Phineas looked just like Penelope, but his hair was more brown than black. The baby boy looked dashing in his green overalls set and striped bow tie. David made cute babies, but Sawyer was surprised at the amount of hair the two had. His three had been little baldies.

"Come on. Let's get them inside. I take it from all the cars out here that we have company?" Sawyer watched Harry run back and forth between the babies.

"You'll see, Dad. Don't ruin the surprise," Ryder said, gently carrying Finn.

Sawyer had a feeling his older omega son was going to spoil his younger omega son. He'd have to make sure Harry didn't get left out. His sweet beta boy was used to being the youngest.

They walked in the house and were met with half the town. The Wilson family was there, of course, but so were all their friends.

Ray and Carter waved from the kitchen door. They had plates of food in hand.

A very pregnant Elijah rushed forward, making grabby hands. "Hand her over, Sadie."

Sadie gently transferred Penelope to Elijah.

"Why, hello, Elijah darling," David said, giving the man a peeved look. "It's good to see you too."

"Oh hush, you," Elijah said. "I'm busy with this beautiful little girl. Look at her, Olive," he said. He looked around for his daughter. "You have to see her, Olive," he bellowed, pushing into the crowd to find his daughter.

"Welcome home," Gramps said, his arm around his wife. "I'm sorry for the intrusion, but we couldn't wait to see the babies."

David hugged the couple. "You two are never an intrusion. The others here?" David shrugged. "It just depends."

The whole Wilson clan had easily transitioned from friends to family. These two loving people had spent more time with Sawyer's kids in six months than their biological grandparents had their whole lives.

"You love us," Grey said, pressing a kiss to David's cheek. He carried Rue and a plate of tamales. "Remember, I'm the one who told Ray your sad backstory and asked him to find Sawyer."

"I'll forever be in your debt, Greyson darling," David said, shooting Sawyer a flirty look. "I love my boo."

"We're going to have so many play dates," Elijah said, returning empty handed to grab Rue from Grey.

"Where did Penelope go?" David asked.

"She's being passed around the room. Last I saw, Carter was cooing over her. I love it when my man turns to mush," Elijah said.

"Here's Finn, Gramps," Ryder said, handing his little brother over. "I held him just like you taught me, but he feels a lot different than Daisy." He turned to Harry, wrapping his arm around his younger brother. "Let's go make sure the nursery looks good. Then we can get some more tamales."

The two ran through the crowd, and Sawyer let a little of his worry go. He had some good boys, and he shouldn't underestimate Ryder. He wouldn't let Harry feel left out.

He watched Gramps and Grammy fuss over Phineas.

David kissed his cheek and linked their fingers together. They wandered through the room, talking and laughing with their friends. It was damn good to be home.

LATER THAT NIGHT, Sadie piled on the couch with the boys, Mo, and Daisy to watch a movie while Cadbury cuddled in the cat bed with Chunky.

David came down the stairs, exhaustion in his eyes. "The babies are finally down. I don't think they'll stay asleep, but we can hope."

Sawyer pulled his man into his arms, burying his face in David's neck, relishing his familiar scent. "I love you, David."

"I love you too, honey buns."

"Can we go upstairs? I need to talk to you a minute," Sawyer said.

"Talk, huh? Is that what we're calling it now?"

Sawyer laughed. "We'll do that too." He peeked into the living room. "Kids, we're going to bed. Don't stay up too late, alright? You all promised to help Grammy pick tomatoes tomorrow afternoon, and Gramps is coming by to take you to Uncle Grey's for the morning, remember?"

"Yes," Harry shouted. "I like riding the ponies."

"Uncle Harper said I could help him in his workshop," Ryder said proudly.

Harper had a woodworking business, and Ryder loved it.

He had even made three little carved figures – a horse, a rabbit, and a dog.

"I'll bring Cadbury, so he can visit the other rabbits," Sadie said. "He needs to learn that Chunky is not his mama. He's a rabbit, but he thinks he's a cat."

"He can be a cat if he wants to, Sadie," Harry said. "Leave him alone."

David shook with silent laughter as the kids argued about whether Cadbury could be a cat or not.

Sawyer shook his head and pulled him upstairs to their room.

The past six months had been the happiest of his life. He loved his kids but having David at his side made all the difference. He even enjoyed his job now. Not that he had hated it before, but he liked it now instead of merely tolerating it.

"What did you want to talk about," David asked, holding Sawyer's hands and spinning them around in circles, grinning like crazy. "Do you want more kids? I admit, the little stinkers are adorable, but I think we're about to become sleep-deprived zombies."

"I think we're okay on kids," Sawyer said, pulling David to a stop. "Stay right here."

He ran to the dresser and pulled open his sock drawer, digging around for a minute. He found what he needed, then ran back to David, dropping to his knee in front of his man.

He held up the open ring box. "Will you marry me, David?"

David's mouth dropped open, and he stared at the vintage, single diamond, ornate engagement ring. "Is that a Tiffany ring? Oh, my god."

"Yes, it is. Someone kept e-mailing me the link to the

Tiffany & Co. website, plus the links for different rings. This specific one was featured quite a bit. The mystery person's e-mail was put-a-ring-on-it-boo@gmail.com."

"Oh, imagine how creative that person must be. He has really good taste too." David grabbed the ring out of Sawyer's hand and slipped it on his finger.

"It's beautiful. I love it," he squealed, spinning around happily.

"So, does that mean you'll marry me?" Sawyer tried not to laugh when David stopped spinning to give him a guilty look.

"Oh, that. Yes, of course I'll marry you. I love you, Sawyer," he said, kneeling with him and kissing him.

Sawyer deepened the kiss and pushed David back, covering him with his body. David's legs wrapped around his hips, and he arched up.

Crying came from the baby monitor sitting next to the bed, and Sawyer groaned. "Cockblockers."

David started laughing and slapped his chest. "You're such a good daddy."

The two got up and straightened their clothes.

They hurried down the hall, splitting up to each take a baby. Sawyer changed Penelope's diaper and absently noted that Carter and Juan had done an excellent job on the nursery.

The walls were wide grey and white stripes. There were pink accents spread throughout the room with a fuzzy pillow on the rocker, a thick rug on the floor, and a pink elephant picture on the wall. Harper had built a double changing table, so the babies wouldn't have to take turns. It was certainly coming in handy.

Sawyer lay Penelope back into her bed and watched

David snuggle Phineas in the rocker. His fiancé slowly fell asleep, a snore escaping him.

Sawyer picked up Phineas and put him back into his bed.

He watched David sleep and thought about the last six months. A year ago, he'd been stressed and lonely, thinking he'd lost David forever. Now, his life was full of love and laughter.

He needed to remember to thank Ray again for his Christmas call. Sawyer knew that he and David had found their happily ever after.

PART II

Bennett's Dream
A Hobson Hills Short
Hobson Hills Omegas: Book 3.5

AUTHOR'S NOTE

"Bennett's Dream" is book 3.5 in the Hobson Hills Omegas series. The events in this short story occur after those in *Romancing the Omega*.

7

BENNETT

ennett Wilson rocked his infant, omega son, singing "Lullaby and Goodnight." He remembered his mom singing it to him, and Bennett had sung it to each of his other three kids when they were babies. His mom was gone now, but every time he sang, she was with him again, whether it was a lullaby or a Neil Young song.

"Lay thee down now and rest, may thy slumber be blessed," he sang. He settled Nathanial into his bed and tip-toed out of the nursery. "Goodnight, Pickles," he whispered to the three-legged calico cat curled in a box next to the crib.

He sighed happily after he shut the door. It had been two months since his sweet boy's birth, and Bennett was in Heaven.

"Papa?" Hannah stood in the doorway of her room. It was late, and she was dressed for bed in soft pink sleep pants and a University of Maine t-shirt. His girl already had her future planned out. She was only thirteen, but she knew she wanted to go to the university in Augustus, and she wanted to be a veterinarian.

He kissed her forehead. "Hey, sweetie. What's wrong?"

He had a good idea of what was bothering her, but he wasn't completely certain.

For a while now, he had known his Hannah was hiding something important. He could act all patient and understanding now, but there were many times Marco had to talk Bennett out of charging into her room and demanding to know all her secrets. Bennett's alpha was the patient type, not Bennett.

"Can I talk to you for a minute?" Her sweet, familiar face was full of worry and nerves.

"Of course," he said and followed her into her room, mentally doing a happy dance. Finally. He would know *everything*.

Bennett and Marco's home was large, with five nice-sized bedrooms and a large master bedroom. Now that Shawn had moved out, the house was too empty during the day. Nate was a good baby, but he did sleep quite a bit, and Hannah spent her summer days volunteering with Dr. Grover, Hobson Hills's veterinarian.

It was nice when Grey brought Rue over to visit though. Bennett's grandson was just now crawling and getting to be a handful. Bennett had always loved a loud and crazy home.

His mother-in-law and sister-in-law thought he was insane.

Hannah's room was a mix of chaos, animals, and pink. Her chocolate Lab, Choco, sprawled across the bottom of her bed. One of their cats, Frankie, slept in a bean bag. The Birman's white fur blended into the fabric, and Bennett almost sat on her. Again.

Hannah's hamster, Butterscotch, ran on its wheel, completely oblivious to the humans in the room, and Sheldon, Hannah's turtle, slept in his aquarium, exhausted. His race track spread across her floor from this afternoon.

Hannah sat on her pink and white comforter, and Bennett finally found a chair without a cat on it. "What's up, sweetheart?"

"You know how I've been spending a lot of time with Summer?"

"Yeah," Bennett said. "You two are best friends."

"Well..." Hannah looked so nervous.

Bennett couldn't take it. He moved beside her and wrapped his arms around her.

Hannah sighed and lay her head on his shoulder, closing her eyes. "She's my girlfriend."

"Okay," Bennett said.

"Okay? That's it?" Hannah lifted her head and stared at him worriedly. "You don't mind? Do you think Dad will care?"

"Sweetie, we love you," Bennett said. "Both of us do. Your dad and I have suspected it for a while, and we're pleased that you're happy and self-aware." He smiled as he said the words Marco and he had practiced. "She's a good girl too. You did well for your first girlfriend."

"She's not just my first girlfriend," Hannah said. "We're in love."

"It's like that, is it?" Bennett asked, eyes wet. Aww, his little girl was in love. "I won't try to tell you what you're feeling, sweetie, but I do want you to be cautious. You're both only thirteen. Mistakes are something you *will* make."

"I know," she said, shrugging. "It's what's happening though. You and Dad met in high school. You both always told me that I'd know when it was real."

Bennett grinned, blushing at the memories of late nights, sneaking out, and dates in the dark movie theater in town.

"Yeah, we did," he said. "We were really lucky."

"Summer and I are like that," Hannah said, nodding firmly. "It just is. I'm going to be the veterinarian in Hobson Hills when Dr. Grover retires, and she's going to create awesome comic books with Jimmy. We're going to live next door in the old farm house."

Bennett grinned. If this was Shawn, he'd shrug and dismiss that childish certainty as wishes and dreams. With Hannah? It was happening.

"Okay," he said. "Just remember, I'm here for you, alright? I love you no matter what."

"Even if I like girls, not guys?" Hannah looked down at her lap. "Summer and I don't know if we even want kids. We'll have so many pets."

"No. Matter. What," Bennett repeated and hugged his girl. Oh, how he loved his family. "You're too young to be thinking about having kids anyway."

"You had Harper when you were twenty," she said, staring him down. "You married Dad when you were eighteen."

"That worked for us," Bennett said. "You don't have to model your life after what we did. It'll happen for you when it happens."

Hannah sighed. "I like having a plan."

"Some of the best things are unplanned, sweetie. If you try to force it, you'll miss out on a lot."

"Okay," she said. She nibbled her lip and looked at him thoughtfully. "There's something else that really bothers me."

Bennett hugged her. "Tell me."

"It's part of why I was worried about how you and Dad would react. When Summer's parents tossed her out, she had to stay at a foster home while the paperwork went through so Yeo could have custody. There was a girl there.

She was trans, and the other kids were really mean to her. Summer said the adults didn't care. She said they told Tali that it was her fault for being weird. Summer told me that they made her go by Robert, because *that was her name*."

"What the hell?" Bennett was pissed. No one deserved to be treated that way, and adults should know better. Kids should know better. Being transgender was tough enough in this society. Add in living in a hostile place? Fuck.

"The adults told her that she'd never be adopted, because no one wanted a freak like her." Hannah leaned her head on Bennett's shoulder. "They didn't call her *her* though. They said she was a boy and needed to act like it."

Bennett's eye twitched. "What's her name and who are her foster parents?"

Hannah's wide eyes met his, and she started to grin. "Should I call Summer?"

"Yes," he bit out, furious. "I'll be back. I need to talk to my cowboy."

Marco

MARCO CLIMBED out of the shower, dried off, wrapped a towel around his waist, and stretched his loose muscles.

Summer time was exhausting. He had three more groups of calves to sell by the end of the month, hay to mow again, and a ton of health checks to make. Plus, the Wilson gardens were producing, so he had to help harvest when he could.

He grinned. Yeah. He loved his life.

"Marco," Bennett said, throwing the bathroom door open.

His omega looked damn fine in his striped pajamas, but his little belly was slowly disappearing. Marco had forgotten how much he loved seeing Bennett pregnant.

Now, though, his omega was upset. Tears filled his pretty green eyes.

"What's wrong, love?" Marco cupped his husband's cheek. If someone hurt his omega, they would pay.

"There's this girl named Tali. She's trans, and her name is *not* Robert." He stomped his foot, then cuddled into Marco's side. "I think she needs me."

Marco listened as Bennett told him about his conversation with Hannah.

Finally, the girl fessed up, he thought. Like they didn't know she was in love with Summer. It was there in her eyes, plain as day, every time she looked at the girl.

Marco kissed Bennett's head as his omega told him about Tali. That poor girl.

"What do you want to do, love?" Marco knew what Bennett wanted. His Benny was a hugging, loving, caregiver. It was who he was, and Marco wouldn't change him for the world.

"She might need us," Bennett said, watching him worriedly. "I don't know what we can do, but I'll check online. I'll see if we can call her too. Maybe having someone to talk to will help. Do you mind?"

"Do I mind us talking to her? No. Do I mind us looking into options to help her? No. Do I mind adopting a kid? Hell no. Whatever you want, love, is what we'll do." Marco kissed his omega's soft lips, Bennett's taste was as familiar to Marco as his own face. It never failed to affect him either.

"I love you, Marco," Bennett said and leaned forward to kiss him again.

He followed his omega to their bed, dropping his towel along the way, and shooed Bennett's big Saint Bernard from the room.

Bennett giggled as he lay back on the bed, naked. He pulled Marco to him. "Poor Oggy."

"He'll be back," Marco said, nibbling Bennett's neck. It was time to love on his omega. He kissed his way down Bennett's neck and chest. He licked Bennett's belly, then moved to his dick. Marco licked him from base to tip, and stroked him up and down. When Bennett's cries were just right, Marco moved on to lick Bennett's hole and stretched him with his fingers.

He eased into his omega's body, reveling in the intimacy of the act. Being inside Bennett was his favorite place to be. Marco held Bennett's legs wide and moved slowly, body heating at the noises his omega made.

They moved together like they had thousands of times before. Minutes later, they both came, mouths joined in a deep kiss.

"I love you, Benny," Marco whispered into his omega's ear, body settling against his husband's.

Bennett cuddled up against him. "Even if I adopt ten kids?"

Marco laughed. "Love, you can adopt as many as you want. Whatever makes you happy." He nuzzled his ear. "I know you, Benny. You have such a big heart."

"You do too," Bennett said, snuggling against him. "How did today go? You got in late."

"We brought two of the smaller herds to the butcher. He'll package it all up and ship it to the grocery stores. Then, we mowed two of the lower fields of hay. We'll fluff and rake it in a couple of days," Marco said, smiling as he thought of the clean air and bright sunshine. He loved working outside. "What about you?"

"I dropped Hannah off at Dr. Grover's, then took Nate to visit Yeo at The Book Worm. Linc read to him. Well, Linc told him a story. It wasn't the book he held at the time." Marco laughed, and Bennett smiled. "After that, Grammy met me at Farm Fresh, and we canned spaghetti sauce for the store." He laughed. "She told me that I would start to feel my age when Nate starts crawling. I think her and Anna are waiting to tell me *I told you so*."

"Bah," Marco said. He got up to let Oggy back into the room, the poor boy scratching at the door. He dived back into bed. "What do they know? Can you imagine life without Nate in it now? I can't. We're in our forties, but we aren't dead. There's nothing I'd rather do than raise babies with you and work the ranch."

"You love babies as much as I do," Bennett said. He kissed his cheek. "Maybe Nate will be the one to take over the ranch."

"Maybe," Marco said, smiling at the thought. "As long as the kids are happy, we're good."

Worry eased the happiness from Bennett's eyes. "What if it comes down to adopting Tali? Adopting will be a lot of work, Marco, and you already do so much. Are you sure?"

"You and the kids are my priority," Marco said. "I love working with the cattle and helping with the gardens, but *you* are what makes me happy. You want more kids? You want to love the whole damn world? Let's do it."

8

MARCO

arco drove toward Dr. Grover's office. Hannah sat in the seat next to him, texting someone Marco suspected was Summer.

He cleared his throat, and Hannah's eyes darted to his. She had been quiet all morning, which was highly unusual. "You okay, baby girl? We haven't talked about what you told your papa last night. You know I love you, right?"

"You don't mind that I like girls or that I'm dating Summer?" Her voice trembled at the end.

"Not at all, baby girl. First, we don't choose who we're attracted too. You can't help it, not that there's anything at all wrong with it." He turned down Main Street, passing by Honey Buns and The Book Worm. "Then there's the fact that we don't really choose who we fall in love with. The day I met your papa, I didn't have anything more on my mind than kissing all the boys and girls I could."

"Then you met him," she said with a grin.

Marco grinned back. "Then I met him, and there was no one else. He was it. I had no choice, not that I'd change a thing even if I did."

"That's how I feel about Summer," Hannah said. "I *liked* Jessica last year, but this is so much more."

Marco shook his head. His kids. "Just be careful," he said.

"That's what Papa said," she blew her bangs out of her face. "Why should I be careful? Isn't a broken heart worth it if I get to love someone first?"

"I don't know," Marco said. He thought of how his sister Anna was when her first husband left. Then came Matt. Poor guy had a mountain to climb. "With luck and caution, maybe you won't end up with a broken heart."

"Fine," she said, rolling her eyes. "I'll see you at dinner tonight."

"Have a good day, baby girl. Don't bring home anymore animals, okay?"

He watched Hannah rush toward the building.

He hung his head out the window. "You heard me, right?"

She disappeared into the building.

She was going to bring home another animal. Damn it.

He drove back through town and stopped at the feed store to load up, then grabbed a cup of coffee at Honey Buns.

His niece Zoe squealed when she saw him. "Uncle Marco! You never come by for coffee. Did Uncle Bennett forget to pack you any today?"

"No," he said, hugging her tight. "He always remembers me. I was taking Hannah to Grover's. I needed some Hannah time."

"Did she finally tell you she's gay?"

"Finally," he said. "Hmm, give me one of those cinnamon rolls too. You make the best, baby doll."

Zoe grinned. "Anything for you."

He left and got to work. His cattle wouldn't tend themselves. It was a pretty day—no rain and seventy-five degrees.

After checking in with his employees, he checked on two of his herds, counting heads, then checked fence in another pasture. He stopped for lunch and called Bennett for some dirty talk. Then he went back to work. Before long, he was pulling into his dad's driveway. He'd promised to help harvest the beets, cabbage, and collard greens.

He knew Bennett would be gathering the first of the blueberries today at their place. Summer was a busy time.

"Hey, Dad," Marco said. His dad was *Gramps* to everyone but his kids and his wife.

Gramps grinned. "Son." He patted Marco on the back. "Ready for some work?"

"Always," he said, and jumped in, working next to his dad. They moved along the rows of vegetables in peaceful silence, filling their baskets.

"How is Nate doing?" Gramps asked, breaking the silence after a while. "Your mama wants to take him a night next week if you boys don't mind."

"That should be fine. I'll check with Bennett to see which night would work best," Marco said, gently cutting a head of cabbage free. "Nate is doing just fine. Spit up all over me this morning, just like babies do."

"You seem to be getting plenty of sleep," Gramps said.

"Bennett and I alternate nights," Marco said. "Last night was my turn to sleep." He grinned. "Truthfully, Nate is the easiest baby we've had so far. He's a good boy. One of the cats, Pickles, even comes and gets us most times when he wakes up. I think I've used the baby monitor maybe once since he was born."

"Good. At your age, you need an easy baby," Gramps said.

Marco frowned. "We aren't that old, Dad."

Gramps looked sheepish. "Sorry, son," he said. "Your mama and I were talking last night about how you boys are at an age to start enjoying your freedom again. We were surprised when we found out Bennett was pregnant."

"Freedom," Marco mused. "Do what you want, when you want, right?"

"That's what I hear," Gramps said, setting another full basket of greens aside and grabbing an empty one.

"Dad, we *are* doing what we want, when we want," Marco said, harvesting another cabbage head. "I love working the ranch, and Bennett was born to be a daddy. It's not that we don't make time for ourselves, because we do. It's just that what we want to do is be busy parents. I don't really see Bennett and me traveling the world. We're happy where we are."

"Hmm," Gramps said.

"Do you ever regret taking in Elijah?" Marco's oldest brother, Stephan, was an asshole. He and his wife abandoned his son when they discovered Elijah was an omega. Gramps and Grammy had taken him in, no hesitation.

His dad looked startled. "What kind of question is that? We love our boy."

Marco nodded. "Just last spring you offered to take in another baby too. Remember?"

Gramps grinned. "I see what you mean." He shook his head. "Elijah was a blessing to us. We would never regret the time we spent raising him."

"Bennett and me just happened to create our little blessing," Marco said.

He wanted to tell his dad about Tali but didn't want to argue with him. He had no idea how his mama would react to them taking in another kid.

"I get it," Gramps said. "Your mama worries, but I get it."

"You know that's why we waited so long to tell everyone about the pregnancy," Marco said. "Worry is one thing, but disapproval is another. We were both feeling pretty judged."

"We don't want you boys to feel like that," Gramps said.

"Then trust us," Marco said. "Trust us to know what is best for our lives."

Gramps eyed him, before setting another full basket down. "Why do I have the feeling you two are up to something?"

"Sorry, Dad. I can't hear you," Marco said, jogging to the other side of the garden. If it worked for Hannah, it would work for him.

Bennett

BENNETT AND HIS BEST FRIEND, Yeo, sat in their window nook at The Book Worm. Nate rocked slowly in his carrier with Linc sitting beside him, holding his daddy's pet, an Angora rabbit named Huckleberry. The little boy was telling Nate a new story. This one involved bunnies and vampires. Hmm.

Bennett and Yeo both stared at the screen of the laptop. "That just seems so complicated. I just want to take care of her, and she needs someone to take care of her. Why does it need to be hard?"

"I guess they need to make sure each child goes to a

good home," Yeo said. "So it looks like the first step is to talk to her social worker. Then, maybe get qualified to be foster parents?"

"Yeah," he said, disappointed. He wanted to go get Tali and bring her home. He told himself to calm down. He had never even talked to the girl.

"Why don't you go ahead and call? We have the number from the agency."

Bennett took a breath. "Okay." He grabbed his phone and dialed the number.

"This is Regina Shackles, how can I help you?"

Bennett sat up straight. "Hi, Ms. Shackles. I live in Maine, but was interested in possibly adopting a child in your care. Her name... I mean his name... Damn it, no. Her name is Tali Jones."

He winced at Yeo's scrunched up face. Yeah, that probably wasn't the best first impression.

"Your name?"

"Oh. Bennett Wilson. My husband's name is Marco. My daughter is friends with a girl who is friends with Tali."

Yeo shook his head and mouthed *keep it simple.*

"Okay," she said. "Tali is a difficult case. She's been in foster care her whole life, and this is the first time anyone has talked about adopting her. Have you spoken to her?"

"No," Bennett said. "I didn't want to overstep myself. I just know she's trans, and she's had a lot of difficulty at her current home."

"Here's what we'll do," Ms. Shackles said. "I'll e-mail you the process for adopting out of state. You work on getting through that process. As soon as we are assured you are potential parents, we'll arrange a face chat between you two. Alright?"

"Okay, yes," Bennett said excitedly. "We'll do whatever you need."

"Good to hear," she said. Bennett could hear the amusement in her voice. "I can tell you the first step to make this process easier is to qualify as foster parents. I'll e-mail you everything now."

Bennett told her his e-mail address and hung up. He stared at Yeo.

"Marco and I are really doing this," he said in awe. "We're doing this."

"Do you feel any regret or a feeling of suffocation?" Yeo eyed him.

"No," Bennett said, shaking his head. "I'm excited. We're doing this."

"Good," Yeo said, smiling.

Bennett took a deep breath. "Okay, so I took over our whole visit with my drama. How are you doing today?"

Yeo rolled his eyes. "You don't know the meaning of drama. Ray is after my papa."

"What?" Bennett tried to hide his smile, but Yeo saw it.

"Smile all you want, but Papa needs time to adjust and heal. His alpha was a son of a bitch, and a person doesn't just bounce back from that," Yeo said.

"Marco says he's really good with the horses," Bennett said. Marco had hired Yeo's papa as a favor, but the man had become indispensable. He took care of all the work horses, pregnant heifers, and hurt or sick cattle. Anything that stayed in the barn was under his care.

"He loves working with Marco," Yeo said. "He's also been working with Noah to set up his horse therapy ranch. They'll be ready to go by September."

"Hannah said he helps Ernie with his alpaca herd too," Bennett said. "Hannah helped them harvest hair last time."

"He loves those damn alpacas," Yeo said. "He's been talking about getting his own."

Amy waved at them from the register and tapped her watch.

"Shit. I have to do inventory. Jackson has tonight off, so I need to get it done before I take over for Amy."

Bennett grinned. "Okay. I'm going to go. I have some blueberries, raspberries, and strawberries to pick and can today."

He looked down at Nate. "Come on, buddy. Say bye-bye to Linc."

Linc waved at the baby, then took one of Nate's hands and waved back at himself. "Bye-bye," Yeo's son said.

Bennett hugged Yeo and Linc, said goodbye, then drove to the garage where Shawn worked. He was starting some college courses online this fall, but he loved his boss's shop. Bennett rolled Nate's carrier inside the business area.

"Mr. Wilson," George, Shawn's boss, said. "Nice to see you and little Nate. You bringing your son some lunch?"

"Yes," Bennett said, handing over a small cooler. "There's enough in there for three."

"Well now, there just so happens to be three folks that work here," George said. "Hang on and I'll go grab him. He's due a break."

A few minutes later, Shawn came out with freshly washed hands and a big grin. His boy was growing into those dang shoulders.

"Hey, Papa," Shawn said, then bent down to kiss Nate's forehead. "Hello to you, little man."

"I brought you and the boys some lunch," Bennett said. "You're going to be at the house Sunday night for dinner, right?"

"Yes, sir," Shawn said with a salute. "I'll also be at Grammy's house for Sunday breakfast."

"Bring Becca if you want," Bennett said. Shawn's girlfriend was leaving for MIT at the end of the month. They had decided to try a long-distance relationship.

"Okay," Shawn said, blushing.

A customer walked in the door, so Bennett gave his son a kiss and left him to work.

"Come on, Nate," Bennett said. "It's time to pick some berries. We'll put your shade up and change your diaper first, huh?"

Back home, Bennett got Nate ready, then headed for the door.

A little squeak stopped him outside Hannah's room. He looked in, and Butterscotch caught his eye. The little guy had his tiny paws plastered against the side of his cage. He squeaked again.

"Okay, Butterscotch," Bennett said. "You can come with."

He put him in his hamster ball with the handle and handed him to Oggy. His big boy loved carrying Butterscotch around.

He picked up Nate's carrier and went outside, followed by Oggy, Butterscotch, Choco, Frankie, and Pickles.

"I'm the pied piper," Bennett said, rolling his eyes.

Bennett and Marco's two-story was in the middle of three acres and surrounded by pasture and woodland. A small barn with their horses stood in one corner, and in another, they had their own fenced-in garden that Bennett took care of. That wasn't where he was headed today.

About ten years ago, Marco had planted Bennett a berry patch. His alpha loved jam, so it was really for his own benefit. Bennett smiled and hummed as he carried Nate to the bushes. They were dripping with berries. He'd make plenty of jam for Marco and Farm Fresh.

He set Nate down and Pickles curled up next to his carrier. The others sprawled around or explored the wood line.

For the next hour, Bennett picked berries and thought about Tali. What kind of person was she? How old was she? Did she like the country or was she more of a city person?

"Ugh, Nate. I'm going to drive myself crazy. We'll fill out paperwork tonight and then wait."

His son watched him with big green eyes. Bennett smiled at him and started singing Neil Young's "Harvest Moon," swaying back and forth as he filled his basket with raspberries.

They'd figure it out.

9

BENNETT

A month and a half later, Bennett sat on the couch, Marco's hand in his. It felt odd to have his alpha home at ten in the morning, but that was when their social worker made the appointment for the home evaluation.

Rachel Little sat in a chair across from them, looking over her notes. Butterscotch rolled into her foot in his hamster ball, and Bennett cringed.

Ms. Little redirected the ball with her foot, without looking up. "You two have seriously moved fast," she said. "You finished your training last week. All your background checks and individual interviews are done as of today." She looked up from her notes. "Your home is wonderful. It helps in a lot of ways that you have children of your own, so this isn't your first rodeo."

"Did we pass?" Bennett was so damn nervous. They still hadn't been allowed to talk to Tali. If things went well today, they would be able to call her tonight.

"Yes," Ms. Little said. "I know you have a girl to bring

home, so I'll push the paperwork through as fast as I can. You are good to call her tonight."

She handed them a sheet of paper with Tali's foster home's number on it. "Tali is eligible for adoption, so after she's stayed here for a little bit to ascertain you are all a good fit, it won't be a hard process." She stared at each of them for a moment. "You have five spare beds in this house."

"We do," Marco agreed, confusion on his face. Two of the three empty rooms had bunk beds.

"I know you plan on adopting Tali, but there are a lot of kids that need a safe place to stay. I hope you'll still be open to fostering after Tali has been adopted."

"We will," Bennett said firmly. He wanted every room in the house filled.

Ms. Little grinned. "Good." She stood. "I'll start processing this paperwork, and I'll keep you updated on Tali."

Bennett and Marco followed her to the door and waved goodbye as she left.

Marco shut the door and grabbed Bennett, spinning him around. "We passed!"

"We can talk to Tali tonight," Bennett said. "We'll call her at seven, okay?"

"We can't talk to her earlier? Ms. Shackles said she gets home from school at 3:30," Marco said, frowning. "Why do we have to wait?"

"I thought you had some things to do today?" Bennett laughed when Marco's new dog came to the door, wagging its fancy, pom-pom tail.

Marco rubbed Honey's silky ears. The standard-sized poodle was always eager to get to work. She was a ranch dog, even with her pretty Dutch hair-cut.

"Honey and I were going to check on some fences, but

we'll be back in plenty of time to call her at 4:00," Marco said.

"Okay," Bennett said, amused at the sight the two made. The big, handsome cowboy and his fancy white poodle.

Marco gave him a mock scowl. "Don't look at us like that. Honey is the best ranch dog I've had in a while. For once, I'm glad Hannah brought home another animal."

"A ranch dog I have to take to the groomer every month," Bennett said with a laugh. "Go on. You two get to work. Nate and I are running to the store to help Anna can the last of the corn. I may make up some zucchini bread to sell too. We'll see."

Marco leaned over and kissed Bennett. "Yes, sir. We'll be back in time to clean up."

He watched his alpha grab his hat and head for the door, Honey at his heels. Bennett chuckled all the way to Nate's room. He fed his sweet boy and put him in a cute outfit. His little shirt was a gift from their nephew, Elijah. It was covered in llamas.

"Your daddy and his poodle are the most adorable thing I've ever seen, Nate," Bennett said. "Well, except for you of course."

He checked on their animals, then drove across the road to the family store, Farm Fresh. Anna was cutting corn from the cobs in the small kitchen in the loft above the store. She stopped to coo over Nate. "Hey there, cutie."

Bennett grinned. "Hi."

Anna rolled her eyes. "Wrong cutie." She went back to the pile of corn and started working again. "How are you and Marco doing?"

Bennett wiggled in happiness and washed his hands. "We are fantastic!"

He hesitated for a minute, then told Anna about Tali.

"Wow," she said. "That's crazy admirable, Bennett, but fostering or adopting a teen will be hard work. She isn't going to be well-adjusted and self-confident like Hannah or my girls. She'll need your support constantly. Are you sure you and Marco want to take on that responsibility?"

Bennett gave her a flat look. "This is why you didn't find out about Nate until I was five months pregnant."

Anna shot him a hurt look. "I'm just trying to be realistic, Bennett."

"Sometimes your realistic and my realistic are two different things," Bennett said. "Do you think Marco and I haven't talked about this? That we haven't thought about the difficulties? We went through ten training classes over the past six weeks."

"Seriously? Marco was able to manage that?"

"Yes," Bennett said, eyes gentling. His alpha had made the time and pushed himself to exhaustion to give Bennett what he wanted. "Marco is fully onboard. This isn't something I'm pushing him into out of loneliness or boredom."

"I never thought that," Anna said. "I guess I just thought of what I would want in your place. Matt and I plan on doing some traveling when Milly and Allison move out. The thought of having a baby right now gives me the hives."

"I would have a baby every two years if I could," Bennett said. Unfortunately, his body hadn't cooperated with them.

Anna winced. "Don't get me wrong. I love my kids, but hell no. I blame it on having twins. Janelle and Evan were little terrors. I'll be happy with grandchildren if Evan and Janelle ever settle down."

Bennett laughed. "Shawn and Hannah were both a little wild. Harper was an angel." He looked over at Nate, sleeping soundly in his carrier. "So far, Nate has been an easy baby."

He grabbed another ear of corn.

"We know what we're getting into, Anna. It would really help to have everyone's support instead of a list of reasons we shouldn't adopt Tali or foster children. Tali doesn't need to think the family doesn't want her around. Even if it's unintentional."

His sister-in-law sighed. "You're right. We never meant to hurt you all. Mama and I are a bit stubborn, and we both got the notion in our heads that you two were making a huge mistake with Nate." She smiled sheepishly. "I'll talk to Mama tonight. We'll do our best to hush up and be supportive. We love you guys."

Bennett smiled. "We love you too," he said. "Now, let me tell you about Marco's new ranch dog."

Marco

MARCO AND HONEY paced the floor in the living room.

Bennett had the laptop turned on, ready to go, but Harper and his omega, Grey, had shown up with their son, Rue. Then Shawn had pulled into the drive, still wearing his coveralls and covered in grease. Then Hannah had skipped theatre practice to come home early.

Hannah and her brothers stood in front of them, all wearing identical stubborn expressions.

"Tali is going to be our sister. We're sitting in on the first conversation so she knows she has our support," Hannah said.

"So many people may make her nervous," Bennett said.

"It may make her feel better too," Shawn said. "She'll know that we all accept her."

"Fine," Bennett said, sighing. "We may as well bring Nate and all the damn animals too. Let's show her what she's getting."

The three siblings grinned and set out to get everyone ready.

Marco grabbed Bennett, cuddling his omega. Having Benny in his arms always calmed him right down. He nuzzled his husband's ear. "Love, your kids are a pain in the ass."

"My kids? They're your kids when they get all stubborn." Bennett kissed his cheek. "Are you as nervous as me?"

Marco swallowed hard. "Yeah. I didn't expect this feeling. What if she doesn't like us?"

Bennett kissed his chin. "Then we'll help her in other ways."

"Enough of that now." Harper came back into the room with Nate and Pickles. Grey followed behind with Rue and Oggy. "You two are way too cozy for our fragile minds to handle."

"Did Zoe tell you about catching Uncle Barry and Uncle Jamie in the kitchen the other day," Shawn asked, nose wrinkled in disgust. "I thought old people were boring."

Marco grinned, then kissed Bennett deeply, bending him backward over his arm. He enjoyed the sounds of displeasure coming from his kids, but soon enough, he got lost in Bennett's taste. Damn, his omega tasted good.

"I'm calling Tali right now," Hannah said loudly. "If you want her first impression of you to be two old people making out, do continue."

Marco pulled back. "She is your daughter when she acts like that."

Bennett grinned. "That girl is all yours. Nate is mine."

"Come on, you two," Shawn said, pushing between them. "Hannah's calling her now."

They all gathered around the computer, each person holding a baby or a cat. The dogs squished between them, Oggy holding Butterscotch in his hamster ball.

A young, African-American boy's face popped up on the screen. His big brown eyes were so damn vulnerable.

"Hi, I'm Robert. It's nice to meet you... all?" His eyes darted from face to face. "Is that a hamster?"

"Robert?" Marco frowned. "I thought you preferred Tali."

The boy met Marco's eyes, and his lip trembled. Marco felt his heart break. "No. I... I can be Robert. I really want to go live with you all in Maine."

He looked nauseated.

Marco fought his tears and gave him a hard look. "If you want to be in our family, then you will be. No strings attached. We would like honesty from you though. We want you to be happy, and that means no masks, sweetheart. Now, are you Robert or Tali?"

"Tali," she wailed, tears streaming down her face. "I hate Robert. I'm *not* Robert."

"Okay," Bennett said, gently. "Then it's a pleasure to meet you, Tali."

Their girl slowly composed herself and wiped her eyes.

"This is our eldest son, Harper, and his omega, Grey. They have a little boy named Rue," Marco said.

"Hi," Tali said, sniffling. She wiped her eyes again and gave Harper and Grey a shaky smile.

"Hey," Harper said. "We can't wait for you to come home."

"Do you like comics? What kind of movies do you like?

What about rabbits?" Grey bounced Rue on his knee and peppered Tali with questions.

"Hey, wait until we're all introduced," Hannah said, nudging Grey in the side. She looked at Tali. "I'm Hannah, Summer's girlfriend."

"She talks about you a lot," Tali said with a grin.

Hannah blushed and cleared her throat when everyone laughed at her. "This is Papa's dog, Oggy, my dog, Choco, and Dad's dog, Honey. Then there's Frankie, Pickles, Butterscotch, and Sheldon." She held up her turtle.

"There's also me," Shawn said dryly. "Hi, Tali. I'm Shawn, and I'm more important than the pets. Well, except for Honey." He leaned forward, grinning. "Honey is Dad's ranching dog."

"She looks like a poodle," Tali said, confused.

"She is," Shawn said. "My boss, George, drove past Dad and Honey working in the field yesterday. He about died laughing, but he said Honey was really good at herding cattle."

Tali giggled, eyes shining.

"Ha, ha," Marco said. "Anyway, Tali, I'm Marco, or Dad to the kids." He threw his arm around Bennett. "This is my Benny, aka Papa."

"Hi, Tali," Bennett said, eyes shining with joy. "I can't believe we're finally getting to meet you. Oh, and this is the youngest of the kids, Nate." He held Nate up so she could see him.

"Okay," Hannah said. "Introductions are over. Now, what *do* you think about rabbits?"

10

MARCO

Bennett sang along to Neil Young from the passenger side of the Jeep, and Marco grinned. They had been in this exact position thousands of time. Him driving them along, Bennett singing his favorite songs. The two babies in the backseat were just the newest audiences to the traditional Benny concert.

They drove down Interstate 65, followed by another Jeep carrying Hannah, Harper, Grey, and Shawn. The kids had insisted on coming with them to pick up Tali.

Bennett leaned over to turn down the radio. "How far away are we?"

"Three hours," Marco said, stifling his smile.

"You said three hours last time I asked," Bennett said, pouting.

"It was three and a half then," Marco said. "I rounded down."

"Ugh," Bennett said. "I can't wait until we get there."

"I know, love," Marco said. "We've talked to her every single night, and the paperwork is finally finished. You aren't the only one that's excited."

"I'm so happy that's she comfortable around us now," Bennett said. "She wears her makeup and her frilly, girly clothes."

"Did she show you her plaid shirt?" Marco asked. "Her foster brother bought it for her at Goodwill. She said that she needed it for helping me with the ranch."

He grinned. Tali had been so excited to show it to him. He loved that girl so damn much.

Bennett laughed. "That's awesome." He turned around. "You have some competition for the ranch, Nate. Don't worry. You have a plaid onesie." He paused for a minute. "Wait. Why plaid?"

Marco shrugged. "I don't know. She seemed excited about it though."

"I love you so damn much, Marco Wilson," Bennett said, shaking his head. His words were familiar, but every time Marco heard them, they sent a shot of warmth straight to his gut. "This is... This is everything to me."

"To us both, love," Marco said and took his hand.

Bennett smiled, turned up the music, and sang along to "Don't Let it Bring you Down."

Right about three hours later, they pulled up in front of Tali's foster home. Regina Shackles sat on the front porch with Lily, Tali's foster mom. The woman wasn't a monster, but that was the best Marco could say of her.

Her face soured as they climbed out of the Jeep.

"I can hit her, right?" Bennett unbuckled Nate from the car while Marco got Rue.

"No, love. You have to behave," Marco said, grinning.

The kids pulled in behind them and unloaded. Grey had insisted on bringing his dog, Chewie, and the big dog dropped down from the back.

Grey rushed over and took Rue and Nate. "I have a feeling you two are going to need your arms."

They started up the walk and the front door slammed open.

Lily's face grew even sourer, but Marco didn't give a damn. There was his girl.

Tali had just turned fourteen last month. She was a slender thing, with long legs and narrow shoulders. Her black hair was cut close to her head, and she wore big, silver hoops in her ears. Marco thought she looked pretty. She was dressed in blue jean shorts and a grey and pink, scoop necked sweater. She squealed and ran down the walk in her black, heeled boots.

"Dad," she said. "Papa!"

She threw herself in Marco's arms, and he held her tightly. Tears pricked his eyes. He was finally bringing her home. He released her so she could hug Bennett, but he couldn't keep his eyes from her.

That's how he noticed the bruises on the back of her neck.

"Tali, sweetheart," Marco said. "Where did you get those bruises on your neck?"

Bennett pulled back and looked at the bruises. His eyes filled with rage. "Who hurt you? Those are finger marks."

Tali shrunk right in front of them, her vibrancy gone. "It doesn't matter. I'm going home."

"Tali," Bennett said, pulling her into a hug again. "We love you so much."

"It's just the boys here," she whispered, her head on Bennett's shoulder. "They don't mess with me if I'm Robert, but when I'm me, they're mean. Ms. Lily says it's my fault. We're leaving here, though, so it doesn't matter."

"I swear, Tali," Marco said, trying to get his anger under control. "We will do everything we can to make sure no one ever hurts you again."

"Tomás used to make them stop, but he turned eighteen last week, and Ms. Lily made him leave. He isn't even finished with school yet," Tali said. "He said he didn't care anyway, but I know he wanted to stay until you all got here."

Marco scowled. He liked Lily less and less the more he heard about her.

"Should they really be hugging him like that?" Lily walked with Ms. Shackles, stopping where they were. "It doesn't seem appropriate – two gay men hugging a young boy."

Marco and Bennett looked at her in silence, their disgust clear.

Marco turned to Ms. Shackles and held out his hand. "It's nice to finally meet you, ma'am. Thank you so much for helping us connect with our daughter."

Ms. Shackles smiled. "It's been a pleasure. I know this will be a good fit for Tali."

"Hey, Tali," Harper said, holding out his arms for his hug.

"Harper! You came too?" She hugged him.

"We all did," Hannah said. She held Chewie's leash.

Tali hugged her and Chewie both.

"Shawn? You aren't covered in grease," Tali said and hugged him.

"I miss it," Shawn said, giving her a squeeze. "Where's your stuff? I don't like the way that lady keeps looking at you."

"Do you guys want me to take her out?" Grey would have looked fierce, except he carried two babies, and he wasn't exactly ferocious.

Shawn snickered. "I would pay to see that."

"Simmer down, sunshine," Harper said, a smile in his voice. "Let's get our Tali out of here."

"Ms. Shackles," Marco said quietly. "Would you go inside with us to get Tali's things?"

The social worker eyed Lily. "That would be a good idea."

"It'll just take a second. I'm all packed," Tali said.

Marco, Bennett, and Ms. Shackles followed her into Lily's house. Shawn and Harper came in behind them, looking around cautiously.

"I'll need to check her bags to make sure she's not taking anything of mine," Lily said, shouldering past them.

"I'll do that, Lily," Ms. Shackles said, giving her a tight smile.

They reached a room with two sets of bunk beds. The other foster kids were at school today, so at least the room was empty. Tali had two bags and a huge stuffed unicorn sitting next to one of the beds.

"Can I look through them, Tali?" Ms. Shackles waved toward her bags.

Tali shrugged. "Sure."

It didn't take long, and Ms. Shackles declared everything belonged to Tali.

Lily just scowled. Marco wondered what she wanted with a teenager's clothes and books. Tali didn't have any electronics or any valuables. He shook his head.

Shawn grabbed her bags, and Harper grabbed her unicorn.

"She's riding with us, right?" Shawn looked at Marco, eyes questioning.

"No," Bennett said, stomping his foot. "I just got her."

"She's our sister though," Harper said, following them

out the door. "A road trip with siblings is fun. A road trip with parents is a nightmare."

Shawn nodded in agreement. "All Papa listens to is Neil Young. He wasn't even born when the guy was popular. He's the oldest forty-three year old I know."

Tali laughed, eyes twinkling.

She grabbed Bennett's hand. "I'll listen to Neil Young. He may be cool. Who knows?"

"He is *very* cool," Bennett said.

"Fine," Shawn said. "We're taking the unicorn then."

"Just be careful with him," she said. "Tomás got him for me."

Marco pulled Ms. Shackles aside as the others piled into the vehicles. "Tali said that Lily made a boy named Tomás leave last week, because he turned eighteen. Is that legal?"

She frowned. "We were told Tomás decided to leave. Legally, we can't make him stay in the foster home once he turns eighteen."

Marco was quiet a minute. "So it wouldn't be a problem if we found him and brought him home with us too? Since he isn't a ward of the state anymore?"

Ms. Shackles gave him a soft look. "I wish there were more families like yours, Mr. Wilson." She shook her head. "There would be no objection from us if Tomás were to tag along with you."

He nodded. Alright then. Time to hunt down a young man.

He got into the car and started it before looking over his shoulder. "Tali, do you know where Tomás is?"

"He's in school right now," she said. "He stays at a shelter a few blocks from here at night, then stores his stuff in his locker at school during the day."

"Are we going to hang out in a high school parking lot?" Bennett shot him a sly look. "We could send the kids on to get a late lunch while we wait."

Marco could hear Tali's stomach growl from the front seat. He frowned. She shouldn't be hungry.

"Lunch would be awesome," she said. "Ms. Lily didn't let me have breakfast, since I wasn't one of her foster kids anymore."

"Okay," Marco said, taking a deep breath. He couldn't murder the bitch. Bennett would be upset. He pulled out and drove toward the highway. "Do you have a picture of him? We'll pick him up while you all eat."

"Tomás is going to come too?" Tali's stare burned a hole in the back of his head.

Marco had to blink away his tears at the hope in her voice.

"If he wants to," Bennett said.

"He will," Tali said excitedly. "We talked about him coming to Maine after he graduated."

"Tali," Marco said, suddenly worried. "Are you and Tomás...?"

Fourteen was too young for that shit.

"Eww," she said. "No way. He's like my big brother. I've never had anyone to look out for me until I got stuck in Ms. Lily's and met Tomás. I wish I had met him sooner."

Marco drove them to a diner close to the high school and left the kids to lunch. Then Bennett and he hung out across from the high school like stalkers with two babies in the backseat.

We are *weird stalkers*, Marco thought, cringing.

The bell rang and kids flooded from the school.

"Damn. I hope we don't miss him," Bennett said, sticking

his head out the window. "Oh, there he is. He's heading toward the bus stop."

"I'll go talk to him. You stay with Nate and Rue, okay?"

"Sure. Hurry up," Bennett said and gave him a kiss.

Marco threaded through the crowd until he stood next to the towering young man. The young alpha was almost as tall as Marco with big, broad shoulders.

"Tomás?"

Tomás turned around, a puzzled look on his face. His backpack bulged and knowing that was all the young man had made Marco want to hit something.

"Yeah?"

"My name is Marco Wilson. I'm Tali's dad."

A wide smile covered the young man's face. "You guys came to get her today?"

"Yes," Marco said with a smile. "She's having lunch with the rest of my kids. She was really worried about you."

Tomás shrugged. "I'm cool. As long as she gets a good home, I'm a happy person."

"We want you to come with us," Marco said. "Hobson Hills has a good high school, and we have extra rooms."

Tomás looked at him in disbelief. "Seriously? I have nothing, man. Absolutely nothing."

"You have the friendship of my daughter," Marco said. "That means you have my friendship. When you graduate, if you want to go to college, we can help. If you just want a job, I have a ranch and could use another hand."

"Okay," Tomás said, voice small. "I'd like that. A lot."

"Let's go talk to the school and get them to transfer your files to Hobson Hills High," Marco said. "Then you can meet my Bennett. He's waiting in the car with our grandson and son."

Marco had to give Tomás a little push to get him moving. The young man looked dazed.

"One second, I'm worrying about eating tonight," Tomás said. "The next, everything's good. Damn."

11

BENNETT

Bennett's phone pinged with a text.

They were almost home, three days later. They had taken their time and done a little sightseeing on the way. It was Saturday morning, and Bennett knew what was awaiting Tali and Tomás when they got home.

He texted Yeo a reply, then tucked his phone away, trying to look innocent.

"Then Summer said that Mr. Washburn wasn't going to be my biology teacher, and I'm kind of glad, but I think I would be fine with a hard teacher. I really like biology," Tali said.

Their girl chattered the *entire* three days. Bennett grinned. He loved it.

"Is that a horse? I love horses." She plastered her face against the window.

"Those are ours," Marco said. "Each of the kids have a horse, and I have a couple for work."

"They're so pretty," she said.

"Do you know how to ride?"

"No. I've never even petted a horse," she said. "I've always wanted to though."

Bennett kept his excited squeal inside him. Somehow. This was going to be so awesome.

"You'll have plenty of animals to pet and love on," Marco said, sending Bennett a happy look.

"We're here!" Bennett yelled, startling Marco and Tali.

They pulled into the drive way, followed by the rest of the kids. There were a ton of vehicles all around the house, but they had left a path to the garage. Hmm. They needed a bigger driveway.

"That's a lot of cars," Tali said.

"Everyone wanted to meet you and Tomás," Bennett said. He jumped out as soon as the Jeep came to a stop.

"Everyone?" Tali followed more slowly and stood by Bennett as he got Rue from the backseat. Marco worked on Nate's car seat fastening.

"Is that Tali? Come here, sweetheart, and give your Grammy a hug," Grammy said, pulling a startled Tali into her arms.

Bennett grinned. Yeah. Now that Tali was here, there wouldn't be any talk of taking on too much.

"Hurry up, Mama," Anna said. "I want my turn."

"Can we move this lovefest from the garage?" Marco asked, not bothering to hide his laughter when both women glared at him.

Bennett went into the house and found Tomás surrounded by Wilsons. He clutched his bag and stared wide-eyed at the crowd of people. One would hug him, then pass him to the next. Right now, he was in Elijah's arms.

Bennett grinned. He did love his family when they weren't being judgy.

He looked around and spotted Yeo. "Thanks for coming, Yeo."

"Like I'd miss this," the man said. Yeo was almost eight months pregnant, but somehow managed to look perfectly comfortable. He sat in a chair and had a baby in each arm. Elijah's twin boys, Cooper and Connor, were adorable little stinkers. "Linc is upstairs playing with Olive. We got a room set up for Tomás, but Olive insisted it needed her touch. Linc thought he'd help."

"Oh dear," Bennett said. Olive was Elijah's daughter, and she was very well-behaved, but she was a bit eager. Linc was... Linc.

Yeo smiled weakly. "How bad could it be?"

It could be very bad, Bennett thought.

Tali came in, and it was her turn to be passed around the room.

Bennett smiled when her eyes widened at David Bartley. The man loved makeup and feminine clothing. He was also a big sweetheart, so maybe she'd feel a little more accepted.

"Tali," David said. "It is so good to meet you. You're going to be besties with my daughter, Sadie. She already checked, and the two of you have three classes together. She's around here somewhere. Oh my god, I love your earrings!"

"I need to borrow Tomás and Tali," Marco said loudly from the kitchen. "Before you two are both lost to the family, come to the back yard. We have a surprise for you."

Bennett bounced Rue excitedly. "It's time, baby Rue," he whispered.

Rue gurgled and chewed on his fist.

The whole family filed through the kitchen, heckling Grey, Ines, and the other volunteer cooks as they passed them.

Gramps held the reins to two horses in the backyard.

One was a small, dapple grey lady with gentle eyes. The other was a bigger brown and white painted gelding.

Bennett watched Tali's eyes grow huge.

Marco wrapped an arm around her shoulders and another around Tomás. "Bennett and I made an agreement when we had Harper that each of our kids would get a horse of their own. It was something Bennett never got to have growing up, so it's important to us. You don't have to work the ranch with me or anything, but we do a lot of family rides throughout the year."

"Seriously?" Tali stepped forward and tentatively petted the dapple grey's nose. "Is this one mine?"

"She sure is," Gramps said. "Your Grammy and I took them both out for a ride yesterday to make sure they were nice and gentle. They'll be good to you two."

"This is for real?" Tomás stepped forward and stroked the gelding's neck. "I never even thought about having a horse."

"They require love, patience, and attention," Marco said. "You two have plenty of all that, and we'll show you what to do to take care of them."

"I'll take good care of you, girl," Tali whispered to her horse. "I'll be the best human you've ever had. I promise."

Bennett wiped his eyes. "Marco and Hannah will show you all how to take care of them after lunch. Come on back in and meet the rest of the family."

Tali hugged her horse's neck, then followed everyone back into the kitchen.

Tomás stayed with his horse a minute longer, petting his soft nose before saying goodbye.

Bennett took the chance to get his attention. "Tomás, I'll show you your room, and you can drop your bag off. I know

Grey and his abuela are cooking up some yumminess in the kitchen."

Tomás smiled shyly. "Okay."

He followed Bennett inside the house and up the stairs.

Bennett opened the second door on the left. They walked in, and Olive jumped from behind the door.

"Surprise," she said loudly.

Linc followed behind her. "Prise!"

"Tomás, this is Elijah's daughter, Olive, and my best friend Yeo's son, Linc," Bennett said, smiling at the kids.

"We put a welcome basket on your bed, Tomás. Linc wanted you to have one of his stuffed bunnies," Olive said, grabbing the young man's hand and pulling him into the room.

A furry, green stuffed rabbit, slightly chewed, sat perched in the pillows of the queen-sized bed. A huge basket full of Elijah's apple products sat at the end of the bed. It looked like there was apple cider, apple bread, some eggs and butter, and a little sampler of apple wine. Bennett rolled his eyes and took that out of the basket.

"Come look in your bathroom," Olive said and tugged Tomás behind her. "Daddy and I made apple smelly soap for the first time last week. I put some right there on your tub. I also left one of my ducks. I hate bath time, but the ducky makes it better."

"Thank you," Tomás said, eyes big and wet. "I can't believe I get my own bathroom, let alone homemade soap and a ducky. I like it, Olive."

"Ernie made you scarves and gloves and hats for winter too," Olive said. "They're in that box on your dresser. He knits real good, but Grey doesn't. We aren't supposed to tell Grey that though. We just say *thank you* and take our presents."

Bennett groaned, and Tomás laughed. "Noted."

"Come on. Let's go get some food," Bennett said. "Remember to help Linc down the stairs, Olive. I'll go put Rue in the nursery."

"Wait," Olive said. "Linc and I have to show Tali her room too."

"I have a Tali right here," Marco said from the doorway. He carried her two bags and the large stuffed unicorn. "Let's go show off her bedroom, guys."

"Tali," Linc yelled and waved as he toddled past her.

Bennett watched Olive and Linc walk Tali through the same process as Tomás, only with a less chewed pink rabbit this time. He took the wine sampler out of her basket too. Looked like Marco and he would have a night cap tonight. Tali's room shared a bathroom with Hannah's room, so Olive had included double the soap and ducks.

"Thank you, Olive and Linc," Tali said and hugged the two. "You guys are the best. Ready for food?"

"Yes!" Olive bounced up and down. "Grey can't knit, but he can really cook."

Bennett rolled his eyes and went to change Rue's diaper and lay him down for a nap.

He and Marco had decided to keep three baby beds in the nursery in case of company, and he'd already used them all at some point over the last month. He smiled when he saw his son was already taken care of and sleeping in his bed. Elijah's twins were together in another and David's twins were in the last bed. Pickles cleaned her fur in her box, standing guard.

"Looks like you're sleeping with your uncle, baby Rue," Bennett said and laid the boy down. He took a moment to enjoy the quiet and watched his grandson settle into sleep. He heard footsteps and turned to find Tomás.

The young man looked around the nursery, smiling when he saw Pickles. He finally met Bennett's eyes.

"Thank you." He waved his hands around. "This. Everything is..." Tears filled his brown eyes. "People like me don't get this."

"People like you?" Bennett took his hand.

"My parents are both in prison. My dad got life for killing a guy, and my mom has five more years left for drug distribution and trafficking. My dad's parents were great, but they died in a car accident when I was five, and my mom's parents didn't want a brown grandson. I've been in the system most of my life. I have nothing. I am nothing."

Bennett grabbed the young man in a hug. "Don't you say that. You are something special, Tomás Hernandez. You're smart and clever, sweetheart. I love seeing you laugh and joke with the rest of the kids. More importantly, though, you're kind. The way you stood up for Tali shows that. You spoiled her rotten with any spare money you had. She told me about the makeup you bought her and, of course, that stuffed unicorn." Bennett squeezed him tightly. "You are a blessing to us, and I plan on showing you that every day."

Bennett held Tomás as he sobbed. His heart hurt for everything this boy had been through. For everything he had never had. He knew that Marco and he had chosen the right path to take.

Tomás and Tali thoroughly proved that.

***

Bennett played with Oggy's ears as he waited for Marco to finish his shower. He was exhausted. It had been a long day, a great party, and a lot of emotional upheaval.

Yeo had insisted on taking Nate for the night so Bennett

and Marco could get some rest, and Bennett was thankful even though he missed his baby.

Tali had settled in quickly and was asleep by ten, Frankie on the pillow next to her. Tomás had a harder time settling in. Bennett had heard him pace back and forth for a while. He'd finally settled down, but Bennett was worried for the young man.

"What's wrong, love?" Marco dried his hair with a towel as he sat on the bed. Honey jumped up and sprawled out next to him.

"I'm afraid Tomás is going to have a hard time adjusting," Bennett said. "He doesn't think he deserves a safe place to live, Marco. What kind of shit is that?"

"We need to offer him stability and security," Marco said, quoting from one of the classes they had taken. "It'll take time, but that's the only way to show both of them that they belong here. We can tell them they do all we want, but they have to *see* it."

Bennett cuddled against Marco's side. His alpha was a smart man. "Okay. I can do that. My heart hurts for him though. I'm going to hug him every day that I can."

Marco kissed his head. "That's a good plan, love."

Bennett snuggled closer. "You know what another good plan is?"

"Hmm, does it involve you and me and this bed?"

"Kindly ask the dogs to leave for an hour," Bennett said primly, pulling his pajama top off.

"Yes, sir," Marco said with a salute.

12

MARCO

Marco shivered as cold air snuck down the back of his jacket. Late fall and winter in Maine was damn uncomfortable, but he still had cattle to tend to. He finished his head count for that herd, happy to note that there were none missing. He had twenty-five pregnant heifers back in the big barn to check on, so he ran a quick check of the fence, unloaded two fresh bales of hay, then drove toward home.

Bennett met him at the barn, holding the phone. "Tali and some others got into a fight with a bully at school. The principal needs us to come in." He bit his lip. "I can go alone, but I thought the two of us together would make a better impression."

"Is she alright?" Marco texted Dean to come check the heifers, then followed Bennett into the house to grab Nate.

"She's fine," Bennett said, huffing out a breath. "Principal Meyers said another kid has been bothering her all week. From what everyone says, the boy catches Tali when there are no adults around and makes nasty comments, and he goes out of his way to pick on her. Until today, she just ignored him and reined her friends in. Today, though, he tripped her in the cafeteria, and she confronted him. He hit her, Marco. The nurse said she was fine, just a bruised cheek, but the little fucker hit our girl."

Marco growled. "What did she do?"

"She didn't have to do anything. Sadie and Allison have lunch with her. Those two kicked the boy's ass. Now, all of them are going to be suspended for a week. Principal Meyers says that's the best he can do. When she first arrived, he encouraged her to come straight to him or a teacher if *anyone* messed with her, but I don't think she believed he'd do something about it."

"Meyers is a good guy," Marco said. "He would have stopped that shit at ground zero."

"Yeah," Bennett said, sighing. He buckled Nate into his car seat and got into the passenger side of the Jeep. "At least Hannah and the others don't have the same lunch time. They would have been in the thick of it too."

"True," Marco said. "So how are we going to do this? Are we mad because she didn't go to Meyers or are we understanding and proud of her for standing up for herself?"

"I think we need to mix the two," Bennett said after a moment. "Encourage her to go to Meyers and avoid fighting, but reassure her that she *should* always stand up for herself."

"Parenting is confusing," Marco said with a sigh. He was proud of Tali and her friends, but fighting really wasn't something to encourage. Damn it.

Together they walked down the hall to the principal's office.

"This place always brings back memories," Bennett said when he passed the place where his locker used to be. He stroked Nate's head, thoughtful.

Marco grinned. "Remember all those times we made out in the boy's bathroom?"

Bennett rolled his eyes but grinned too. "That's what you remember most about high school, isn't it?"

Marco shook his head. "Nah. I remember you wearing my coat at football games. It was too big and the sleeves hung over. I remember you helping me with my chemistry homework and refusing to kiss me until I did my assignment. I remember you getting the part of Hamlet in the school play junior year. You were so hot in those tights. I remember you drawing every damn eye when you walked into the cafeteria." He smiled softly, lost in thought. "High-school-you was pretty awesome."

"Do you miss high-school-me?"

"Now-you is even better than high-school-you, so there's nothing to miss," Marco said, shrugging. Bennett was the best thing in the whole damn world. It just was what it was.

Bennett took his hand. "I love you too, cowboy."

They reached the principal's office to find Anna and David both waiting.

David leaned forward in his chair. "Are we upset or proud? I can't decide."

"Both," Anna and Bennett said at the same time. They shared a smile.

"Confusing, right?" Marco sat beside David and stretched his long legs out in front of him. "Where's the other kid's parents?"

"They will be meeting with me separately," Meyers said, striding into the waiting area. "We'll talk here, so your girls and Tommy can stay in the office a bit longer. They need the alone time to talk." He gave them all hard looks. "The school doesn't tolerate fighting for any reason. While I personally applaud Sadie and Allison's actions, there was a better way to handle the situation and they all knew it. Tali, however, didn't throw a punch. She was punched. She wasn't going to be suspended, but she insisted that if her friends were, then she should be too." He looked at Marco and Bennett. "I'll excuse her absences if she insists on staying out too, but I'm not going to suspend her."

"Thank you, Principal Meyers," Bennett said sweetly. Marco stifled his smile. His Benny was such a kiss up.

"Sadie and Allison *are* suspended for a week," Meyers said. "That won't change."

"We understand," Anna said, nodding. She clamped a hand over David's mouth to stifle his curses. "We *do* understand."

"What about Tommy?" Marco asked.

"He is also suspended and will have detention every day for the rest of the school year on top of that," Meyers said.

"Why aren't his parents here with us?" Bennett asked curiously. Marco wondered the same thing. Unfortunately, they'd been in this position before with Shawn.

Principal Meyers sighed. "To be honest, Tommy learns his behavior straight from them. I'm going to have to wear my extra stern face with them, and I didn't have to with you all. If I put all of you together, it will turn into a brawl." He eyed David accusingly.

David gave him an innocent look.

"Now, I'll go get the girls. You all behave while I'm gone."

"Expelled!" David sounded so offended.

At least he waited until Meyers was gone, Marco thought.

"Suspended, you idiot," Anna said. "Where's Sawyer? I'm surprised he sent you by yourself."

Sawyer is much more levelheaded than David, Marco thought.

"I had to beg him to let me handle it," David muttered. "No one trusts me."

"We do trust you, David," Bennett said. "We just also know you."

They were interrupted by the girls. Marco growled when he saw the big bruise coming up on Tali's cheek.

She looked extremely nervous.

Bennett grabbed her and hugged her, all the while whispering reassurances in her ear.

Anna arched her brow and pointed toward the door. Allison kept her head high and marched.

David hugged Sadie, then pulled her out the door, almost running. Marco had to stifle a laugh when the man glared at Principal Meyers on the way out.

"Let's go home, sweetheart," he said. "We'll get some ice on your cheek, then go visit Daisy."

Tali nodded and walked with them to the Jeep. She was quiet the whole way home, only whispering to Nate in the backseat.

Bennett settled her in the living room and ran to get an ice bag.

As soon as she had the ice on her cheek, she looked back and forth between them. "Do I have to go back to Tennessee?"

Marco gave her a confused look. "What do you mean? Do you want to go back?" The adoption paperwork was finished, and they went to court in two weeks. Did his girl want to leave them?

"I caused trouble," she said, mumbling. "Allison and Sadie both got in trouble because of me."

"No," Bennett said sharply. "They got in trouble because they thought with their fists, not their heads. *You* didn't do anything wrong. Tommy whoever-he-is was the one who started this whole thing."

"We would rather you have talked to Principal Meyers when he started bothering you," Marco added. "He's a good guy, and he takes care of his students."

"So I don't have to go back?"

"Never," Bennett said. "This time, you didn't do anything wrong, but even if you had, Tali, we won't ever send you back. You're our daughter, just like Hannah."

"Can you see us sending her to live with someone else?" Marco asked.

"No," Tali shook her head. "You love your kids."

"Just like we love you," Bennett said. He took Marco's hand, squeezing it. "You're a Wilson now, sweetie."

She gave them an agonized look. "You promise? You can't say stuff like that then change your mind. It has to mean something. You have to mean it."

"We mean it," Marco said. "Sweetheart, we mean it." He sat beside her and hugged her. "We love you, and you're ours."

Marco and Bennett's eyes met over Tali's head as she cried. Bennett looked so sad, but so happy. Marco got it. He hated that Tali struggled to understand that she was accepted here, but he damn sure loved being able to be there for her.

After a few more tears, Marco wiped her face off. "Ready to go see Daisy?"

She smiled. "Yeah. My horse is the best. I need to tell her about today."

Marco grinned. That was exactly what a horse was for.

"Tommy is... complicated. Daisy will get it."

Marco lost his smile. He wasn't sure he wanted to think

about Tommy as anything but a little punk. "What do you mean, sweetie?"

"Sadie, Allison, and I had a talk with him in the office." She shrugged. "There's something wrong with his parents. I don't really know for sure. I'm going to be his friend though. Whether he likes it or not."

A fierce light filled her eyes.

"Okay?" Bennett looked at him, confused. Marco couldn't offer an answer. He was confused too.

"Daisy time?" Tali looked to Marco. He nodded and got up.

Bennett kissed her head. "Have fun, sweetie. Nate and I are heading over to Grammy's house to get some fresh milk and butter." He looked at Marco with big, green eyes. "We need a milk cow."

"A milk cow? Next thing you know, you'll want chickens too," Marco said, hiding his smile with a scowl. Of course, he'd get his Benny whatever he wanted.

Bennett winked at him. "That sounds perfect, thanks."

13

BENNETT

A few months later, in early February, Bennett watched Tomás and Shawn shovel the snow from the front walk. He sat on the porch, wrapped up with Nate in a warm, knitted throw, enjoying the cold fresh air.

Tomás' new dog, Mitzy, attacked the large pile of snow the boys had made. The small Havanese-mix disappeared into the pile and all the boys could see was the movement of the snow as she tunneled around.

Shawn bent low, close to the pile, and Mitzy popped out, barking. Shawn screeched and fell back, landing on his ass.

Bennett laughed hard at the sight, enjoying the sound of Tomás' laughter as well as Shawn's disgruntled look.

Tomás had to brace his hands on his knees as he wheezed. "Good girl," he said, crooning to his dog.

"I'm so glad we got him Mitzy for Christmas," Marco said, sitting on the swing beside Bennett. Honey lay down at his feet, her pretty pink and purple sweater keeping her warm. "That dog and Paulo have never been more loved."

Bennett nodded, still laughing. Tomás really loved his

horse and dog. The young alpha was naturally loving and was able to let down his guard with the animals. He was getting better about letting down his guard with people too.

"Uh oh," Bennett said, amused. The boys had decided to settle their differences with a snowball fight. "Are they both really eighteen?"

Poor Tomás was being pelted. He clearly needed practice.

Marco laughed. "Eighteen is the new fifteen, love. Didn't you know that?"

"Dad," Tali said from inside the house. "When are we going to check on the north pasture?" She came outside, dressed to be a winter cowgirl – thick brown coat, blue jeans, brown boots, and a warm pink hat with earflaps. "I'm worried about that herd, because Joey said they had trouble with the fence."

"Did you eat lunch?" Bennett asked her, smiling. Just like Marco, he had to remind her to take a break once she started working. She spent her weekends helping Marco and her weeknights taking care of Daisy.

"Yes, Papa," she said, rolling her eyes. "I ate it all. Dad, come on already. We have work to do!"

Bennett treasured the proud look on Marco's face. His alpha was extraordinarily happy that Tali loved the ranch.

"On my way, sweetheart," Marco said, pushing himself up with a groan. He bent and kissed Bennett. "Thanks for lunch, love. I'll milk your damn cow when I get back, alright? Don't worry about trekking through the snow to get to the barn."

"You don't have to convince me to stay inside the warm house," Bennett said. "Bye, cowboy. Be careful." Bennett watched them go, then looked down. "Have you had enough of this cold, Nate? Let's go inside."

Pickles met him at the door, staring him down.

"I'm sorry I took your baby outside in the cold. You could have come you know."

The cats did not like the cold. Frankie lived next to the fireplace in the winter, and Pickles wouldn't put a paw outside.

He had just settled Nate down for a nap when he heard feet on the stairs. He poked his head out the door. Grammy waved at him, then came to look over Nate.

She counted his toes and fingers. "Yep. They're still all there."

She followed him out of the nursery. Oggy poked his head out of the bedroom. The big dog carried Butterscotch's hamster ball again. Hannah must have set him up before she headed over to Summer's house with Choco.

"Do you have some time? I want to make bread, and it's more fun to bake with family."

"Hmm," Bennett said. "Do laundry or bake bread with Marco's mama?"

"You better choose baking bread with Marco's mama, Bennett-boy," she said, poking his side.

He laughed. "Okay, okay. Come on, woman."

Bennett went downstairs to the kitchen. Oggy and Butterscotch followed, the hamster squeaking the whole way. They started mixing the dough, working well together. He'd made bread with Grammy a thousand times over the years. When Grammy had something to say, she came to make bread.

"I wanted to talk to you," Grammy said.

Bennett hid his smile.

"Seeing you and Marco with Tali and Tomás made me realize what a complete ass I've been, Bennett."

He looked at her in surprise. "You've been nosy and a bit critical, Mama, but you weren't an ass."

"Yes, I was," she said. "I thought you shouldn't have more babies or take on more responsibility, and I let you know about it every chance I got. I was obnoxious, even if it was coming from a place of love. Marco and you are good parents, and you two know what you want in life. You know what you can handle. I'm damn proud of you, Bennett-boy."

"Mama," he said, tears filling his eyes. "Thank you."

"Now, tell me about Harper and Grey. I have suspicions I'm going to be a great-grammy again."

"You aren't the only one with suspicions," Bennett said. "I found Grey throwing up yesterday morning when Nate and I went to visit with him and Rue."

It was Tali's turn to wash dishes, so Bennett made sure to put up the left-over beef stew while Tomás and Hannah cleaned off the table. Marco brought a dirty baby upstairs for a bath. Nate had decided he would try to wear his dinner instead of eat it.

Choco, Mitzy, Honey, and Oggy handled the floor cleanup. They were such good dogs.

"Papa," Tomás said. "Can I talk to you for a minute?"

"Sure," Bennett said, his inner self dancing a jig at being called Papa by Tomás.

They went into the living room and sat in front of the fire place. Frankie eyed them from her cat bed.

"I've been talking to the guidance counselor a lot over the last month," Tomás said. "My grades have gotten a lot better, but I don't know if I want to do college right now."

"Okay," Bennett said. "You have a lot of options. You can

go right into the workforce or develop a trade. You could even go to college later if you wanted to. We need to think of what's best for you."

"I want to train with Carter to be a plumber."

"Oh," Bennett said, sitting up straight. "You already know for sure? That's a good profession to go into."

"I was thinking about joining the Navy, but I don't want to leave Hobson Hills. Not now that I just found you all. What would Mitzy and Paulo do without me?"

"I'll be happy for you no matter which path you choose," Bennett said. "No matter where you are in the world, you're still my son. That being said, I *would* miss you if you left."

Tomás grinned. He looked so damn excited. "I talked to Gramps, and there's a small house on the other side of Harper's place. It has a few acres with it and a tiny barn. Paulo would have his space, Mitzy would have a back yard, and I would be close to you guys. Carter said he'd hire me on part-time until I graduate if I wanted. Then I could train with him full-time and get licensed. He said Juan and him could really use the help. They've been getting work from a lot of the surrounding towns too."

Tears filled Bennett's eyes, and he wrapped Tomás in a hug. "You have a good plan, sweetie. I'm so proud of you."

Tomás hugged him back, squeezing him tightly. "I wish I had found you and Dad earlier," he said. "I guess I needed to be there for Tali though."

"Fate or not, I wish we had you both earlier too." Bennett sighed.

"What did I miss?" Marco settled into the seat next to Tomás. He cuddled a clean Nate to his chest.

Bennett and Tomás filled him in on Tomás's plans.

Marco grinned and slapped Tomás's shoulder. "Already figured everything out? Good job!"

"Papa," Hannah yelled from the kitchen. "You're cell is ringing."

Bennett jumped up and rushed to the kitchen while Marco and Tomás talked about the little house he'd be moving into in the summer. Bennett smiled when Tomás talked about eventually buying it once he got settled into his job. Like Gramps would let him pay for it. The old man was all about making sure everyone had a home, and Bennett had no doubt that he'd already bought it from the family that rented it out.

"Hello," he said, answering his phone.

"Bennett Wilson? This is Rachel Little."

"Oh," he said. "Hi!" His heart thudded loudly in his chest.

"I was speaking with a few of my colleagues yesterday, and one of them mentioned a young beta who was having some trouble at his foster home. He just turned fifteen and came out. His foster parents aren't supportive and have asked that he be moved," she said.

Bennett gasped, horrified at the thought of kicking someone out for their sexual orientation. "We'll take him."

PART III

Justin's Journey
A Hobson Hills Short
Hobson Hills Omegas: Book 4.5

AUTHOR'S NOTE

"Justin's Journey" is book 4.5 in the Hobson Hills Omegas series. The events in this short story occur after those in *Healing the Omega*.

14

———

JUSTIN

"**I**'d like a slice of the steak and ale pie and an order of the loaded pub fries."

Justin wrote down Dr. Grover's order, then smiled. "I'll get that order in. Would you like a pint of Abel's stout with that? They go well together."

"Sure thing," Grover said with a grin and leaned forward on the bar. "Anything Abel brews is good, and that cook of yours is the best."

Justin tapped the top of the bar. "You're not lying, Doc. Are you having dinner with your ladies tonight?"

"I am," Grover said. "They'll make me eat a salad, so I need to get the good stuff now while I can."

Justin grinned. Grover was in a relationship with two widows, and they did their best to take good care of him. That didn't stop him from eating lunch at the pub twice a week.

"Say, you want a guinea pig? He's a cutie."

Justin arched a brow. "I can say no to you, Doc Trickster. Pawn the piggie off on Carter or Hannah."

"You're so heartless."

"Fine. If you come across a unicorn, I'll adopt it."

"You play a mean game, Justin Ames."

He typed the order into the computer, then quickly pulled a pint of the stout and set it in front of Grover. "You know it, Doc."

The pub was packed, which was usual for lunchtime on a Saturday, but it seemed to have stayed packed for the past three weeks. It wasn't even their busy season. The spring was supposed to be their slowest time.

His servers weaved between the tables inside, and the patio was full of customers and their pets. Unfortunately, his new bartender was missing.

Justin refilled drinks and checked on the customers at the bar, then worked on the drink orders the servers gave him. He looked around the room again. No sign of Eddie.

"Justin, Chelsea isn't on the floor." Nell picked up her drinks and gave him a worried look. "She said she needed to go to the bathroom, but it's been twenty minutes, and Laura and I have been taking care of her tables."

"I'll go find her. Eddie is missing too."

"Oh." Nell wrinkled her nose. "I bet they're in the storage room. Chelsea took something on her break, and you know how she is when she does that."

Justin cursed. "Nell, please keep an eye on the front, if you can. I'll be right back. You and Laura will need to split Chelsea's section."

"Damn. Are you finally firing her?"

"Not much choice. We're desperate right now, but not this fucking desperate." Justin checked on each of the customers at the bar one more time, then headed through the kitchen.

The day cook looked up from his grill. Reuben was African American and a giant of a man, huge and muscular, who seldom spoke. Justin and Abel tried their best to get the man to open up and join the community, but Reuben could easily have been a hermit.

They didn't know too much about his history. He came to work and went home; that was it. The quiet alpha even had his groceries delivered. Despite his solitary nature, Justin and Abel both adored the man. He had moved to Hobson Hills a year ago and completely revamped the pub's menu, almost doubling their profits. He was the best hire Justin had ever made.

Reuben gave him a questioning look.

"Are they in the storage room?"

The alpha nodded, looking disgusted.

"I so don't want to do this."

Justin's phone pinged. He looked at Tanner's text and sent a quick reply.

Tanner: Can't come to dinner at the pub tonight. Picked up 3rd shift. I'm an idiot.

Justin: np. luv u. be careful.

That sucked big time. For the past month, Tanner had picked up more and more shifts on top of his normal schedule and his volunteer hours with the fire department. Justin didn't know why he needed the extra money. Tanner was definitely not a big spender.

Justin sighed. His favorite part of the day was when he saw Tanner, and he needed some good today, damn it.

He took a deep breath. "Okay." He filled a pitcher with water and stomped across the room, pausing outside the door. He could hear their moans from there.

He wrinkled his nose and closed his eyes, then opened the door, startling the couple.

"Hey," Eddie said. "Give us a minute, man."

Chelsea giggled, then moaned again.

Justin didn't open his eyes. He tossed the water toward their voices, smiling when he heard them screech.

"You're both fired. Get your shit and get out. I'll mail your final checks." Justin turned and walked back through the kitchen, leaving the pitcher on one of the counters.

Reuben smiled softly and gave him a gentle pat on the back.

"What am I going to do? We only have one other bartender, and the summer tourists will be here before we know it."

Summer time in Hobson Hills was tourist season, and the Irish Rose had proven to be a favored destination last year. With the extra traffic they pulled in due to the yummy food, they would be overwhelmed quickly.

Justin rubbed his eyes. He was so tired, and he knew it would get worse before it got better.

"Got a friend," Reuben said, voice deep and husky. "I'll call him."

"Really? Reuben, that would be so helpful."

"I can't believe you're firing us." Chelsea stomped out of the storage room, clothes askew. Her pupils were dilated, and her hands shook. He recognized the signs all too well.

Justin saw Eddie slip out the back door and shook his head. "This is the second time you've been high at work, and you just got caught having sex on the premises while you're on the clock. Is it really that surprising?"

"You think you're so much better than us," Chelsea snarled and grabbed her purse from her work cubby. "You look at us like we're trash, but you're just like us. You should have seen your mom last night at Wally's party." She smirked. "She was so fucking messed up. Yeah, you're just like the rest of us, Justin Ames. You can pretend all you want. One day, that deputy of yours is going to realize the piece of shit he's been fucking."

Justin felt the blood drain from his face.

"Get out." Reuben's voice was rough, and he took a step in her direction.

Chelsea's eyes widened, and she ran for the door. It slammed shut behind her.

"Justin?"

"She's right," Justin said quietly. "Mom got arrested last year, and Tanner had to bring her in. I was so embarrassed. I'm used to it all now, but Tanner is third generation law enforcement."

Reuben gave him a questioning look.

"Tanner just rolled it off, like it was nothing." Justin bit his lip. "It can't have been easy on him, and one day, he'll realize he won't get far hooked to me."

Reuben glared at him and snorted. "Stupid."

Justin took a deep breath and let it out. He didn't have time for introspection. "You'll see, Reuben. I need to get back up front."

He pushed through the door and checked on his customers. The regulars were kind enough not to comment on his pale complexion or the tears in his eyes.

CLOSING TIME FINALLY ARRIVED. Damn, but they made a lot of money today. If business stayed this good year-round, Justin knew he would have his portion of the business paid off within a couple of years. Then, he would pull in more money each year.

Justin wiped the bar down for the night and checked their inventory one last time. Abel was on vacation in the

Caribbean, so he had brewed extra barrels of beer just in case they ran out while he was gone. So far, so good.

"Hey, boss," Wiley said, grabbing his attention.

Justin turned around and leaned back against the bar. The older beta was Justin's evening bartender.

"I just wanted to let you know, I can help out during the day if you need me to." Wiley waved a hand toward Justin. "You look really worn out. That can't be healthy."

"You'll burn out fast if you work fifteen-hour days," Justin said.

"That goes for you too, boss. Let me help you, so you don't have to work fifteen-hour days. I could use the extra money. Maybe we can alternate until we find someone else."

"I can help out too," North, one of the evening servers, said. "Plus, Laura told me she wouldn't mind working a few long days. It's worth it to have Chelsea gone."

Justin sighed. He really didn't have much choice. "If you all are sure, I could use the help."

"I'll take tomorrow," Wiley said with a wink. "North can work a double too."

North nodded and smiled sympathetically. "Go on to bed, boss. We'll finish closing."

"You guys are the best." Justin handed Wiley the rag, then went to the kitchen.

Albie, the night cook, had closed the kitchen down a few hours ago. Everything was spotless, and a list of what they were low on awaited Reuben for the morning.

Justin unlocked the door leading upstairs and slowly made his way to his apartment. His home was spacious, with three bedrooms and two bathrooms. A large, covered balcony ran along the back and overlooked the thick forest surrounding the pub. The stairs from the kitchen led to the balcony, and he took a minute to look out at the dark, wet night. Rain pelted the roof, soothing Justin's nerves.

So, his mom was taking pills again. She had been clean for two full months, but he had known it was just a matter of time before she was back on them again. He rubbed his face with his hands and tried to force the feeling of helplessness away. He knew nothing would change with her.

Unlocking the front door and entering, he stood in the entryway of his apartment. "Butter Bunny. Are you awake, baby?"

His large blond Angora rabbit hopped quickly toward the door from the laundry room.

Justin knelt and held the rabbit to his chest, pressing his face against her soft hair. A little over two years ago, his best friend, Grey, gave Justin a baby rabbit for Christmas. At the time, Justin had had no idea that Butter Bunny would be his favorite thing in the world. Well, his second favorite thing in the world. Tanner was pretty damn amazing.

The apartment was quiet, and Justin thought again about how much happier he would be if Tanner moved in. Justin's alpha wanted to move in, but Justin kept putting him off.

Justin was afraid to let Tanner in, because Justin *was* a piece of shit – garbage with a pill addicted mom. Chelsea was right. One day, Tanner would realize he was better off without Justin.

Giving up, he finally let go of the pain and worry he had held in all day. Justin sobbed into Butter Bunny's hair and rocked himself back and forth. He could tell himself he was a businessman with a bright future all he wanted, but he was still the boy from the trailer park with the dirty and torn clothes.

The boy whose dad ran off and broke his mom's heart.

The boy whose mom didn't care enough about him to buy groceries. The boy whose mom traded their food stamps for pills, leaving him to go hungry. To look for food in places he didn't want to think about.

Butter Bunny stayed with him, a warm comfort while he cried. Time passed and his tears slowed. He wiped his eyes and set his rabbit down.

"I'm sorry, Butter Bunny. I needed that."

He went to the bathroom and took a quick shower, washing the long day away. As he brushed his teeth, he looked at the plastic stick still sitting on the counter from that morning. Two thick, pink lines clearly showed in the little box.

He spit in the sink and knocked the stick into the trash can. He didn't want to think about it.

15

TANNER

Tanner Jones sat in the hallway outside the morgue at the local hospital. At five in the morning, the hospital was almost empty. There was no one else in the basement.

He leaned his head back against the cold concrete wall and closed his eyes. Pain throbbed at his temples and exhaustion made his shoulders droop.

It had been a long, horrible night, but the worst part was still left to do.

Travis sat beside him and handed Tanner a cup of hot coffee. "I can do it if you want me to. I should probably be there anyway. That way you can focus on him."

"Maybe that would be best." Tears pricked Tanner's eyes.

This was going to devastate Justin. It fucking tore Tanner's heart in two.

Three hours ago, Tanner had gotten a call about a single car accident on Main. The streets had been empty when he arrived, barely beating the ambulance. He'd recognized Rhonda Ames's car right away. Justin had given it to her for Christmas.

"No one wanted this for her," Travis said. "She was a sweet lady, even during an arrest. Damn it. This really sucks, man."

"I just…" Tanner started to say, then stopped.

"What is it?"

"This is going to fuck with his head."

"His mom is dead. I think that would mess with anyone's head."

"I love Justin. I want to be with him for the rest of our lives."

"I know, man." Travis patted his back. "You bought that big ole expensive ring."

"We've been together for over two years, and he won't let me move in. He keeps his emotional distance. You know what I mean? Now, I have to tell him that, after being clean for months, his mom died in a car accident while under the influence of oxycodone. I'm a selfish bastard, but all I can think about is how he's going to push me away."

"The way that man looks at you?" Travis shook his head. "He loves you too, and he will need you. Maybe you're over-thinking things."

Tanner scrubbed his face with his hands. "What the fuck do I know? Justin is good at keeping his feelings a secret."

He stood, drained the rest of his coffee cup, and then threw it away. "I need to think of Justin now, not myself. I got this, Travis. He doesn't like to get upset in front of other people, so I really should do this alone."

Travis stood. "Okay. I'll finish up the paperwork. You know Hobson Hills. This will be all over town by noon, especially considering the damage her car did to that streetlight."

Tanner nodded and hurried out of the hospital. He

drove quickly and parked at the back of the pub. He ran through the rain and jogged up the stairs to Justin's apartment. The two garden gnomes Justin's mom had gotten him for Christmas were perched beside an empty flower pot. Tanner felt tears fill his eyes again and fought them back.

He unlocked the door and slipped inside the silent apartment. It was way too early for Justin to be awake, considering what time he finished up last night, so Tanner went straight to the bedroom.

Butter Bunny slept in a small cat bed next to the bed, and Justin was curled into a ball under the quilt Grammy Wilson had given him last Christmas. His soft blond hair poked out of the top of the blankets. He looked so peaceful, and it tore Tanner apart. He knew he was going to break his man's heart when he woke him. He stared at Justin for a moment, wishing he did not have to do this.

"Justin. Wake up, honey." Tanner sat at the edge of the bed and gently shook Justin's shoulder.

"Hmm." Justin's eyes fluttered open, and Tanner mentally cursed. His omega was as exhausted as he was. "Tanner? Did you come to sleep with me? I could use a snuggle."

Tanner slid in beside his omega and wrapped him in his arms. "I have to give you some bad news, love. Something happened."

Justin blinked, becoming more awake every second. "What's wrong?"

"You mom was in an accident early this morning."

"Is she hurt? Is she in jail? Did she hurt someone else?" Horror filled Justin's eyes.

"She's dead, Justin." He hugged his man tightly. "I'm so sorry."

Justin didn't speak. He lay there in shock for a while, then he cried – long, deep sobs. Tanner held him close and murmured soft, nonsensical words, offering what comfort he could.

A couple of hours passed, and Tanner thought of the woman he had spent so much time with. Rhonda Ames had loved her son, but she had also had an addiction problem. Like many addicts, that addiction always came first, but despite that, Tanner knew she had loved Justin.

Justin loved her too, but he hated the drugs. Tanner knew this loss would hit him hard. There would be no closure between them.

"What happened?" Justin's voice was broken and rough.

"She was driving impaired on Main Street. It rained some last night, so the roads were a little slick." Tanner swallowed hard. "From what we can tell, she swerved and hit a streetlight. The coroner said it was fast."

"Was... Was anyone else hurt?"

"No. She was alone."

"Good." Justin buried his face against Tanner's shoulder, then jerked away. "That stupid, stupid fucking woman. How could she be so selfish?"

Tanner smoothed a hand over Justin's head. "Honey, I'm sorry. I don't know what to tell you."

"Chelsea said mom was at one of Wally's parties last night, so I'd known she'd started using again." He was quiet a moment. "I'd really hoped she had gotten better. I really had hoped."

He started crying again, and Tanner joined him.

"She tried. I know you don't think it, but she loved you so much, Justin."

"Then why did she keep going back to it? Why did she

do something so fucking stupid and dangerous? She could have killed someone else too."

Tanner hesitated, then told him the truth. "After she got arrested last year, she talked to me about rehab."

"What?" Justin's large green eyes were wet with tears.

"I told her about this place I knew of. She talked to them, but didn't check herself in. She decided she would try therapy first."

"She did?"

"We talked a lot. When your dad left, she was depressed. Then, she had a minor surgery and was prescribed pain pills. They made her feel better. She loved the feeling they gave her, the feeling of not feeling anything. When she decided to go clean, she thought that if she dealt with the depression, she might be able to kick the addiction without going through rehab."

"I never realized you two talked so much."

"I'm in love with her son. She wanted to make sure I was good enough for you."

"Good enough for me? Shouldn't it be the other way around?" Justin shook his head. "Never mind. So, she went to see someone?"

"Yeah. I know she was talking to Dr. Woodward for the past five months. She wanted to be the one to tell you, so I never said anything. I figured you two would talk in time."

"She was clean until recently."

"Addiction isn't something that goes away, love. Once the pattern is established, it's always there. She was trying, and she wanted to live, to be with you. That's what you need to focus on."

"I don't know. I need to think." Justin climbed out of bed, and Tanner moved to follow him.

"No," Justin said, shaking his head. "You need sleep, and

I need to be alone to think for a little bit. I'm going to get dressed and drive around. Clear my head."

"Can I come with? I'll be quiet. I really don't want you to be alone right now."

"I need to be alone." Justin cupped Tanner's cheeks. "I love you, Tanner. I just need to think right now."

He pressed his lips to Tanner's, and he could taste the salt from his omega's tears. Justin pressed another kiss to his mouth. Then another, before reluctantly letting him go.

"I love you, Tanner Jones."

"I love you too, Justin Ames." Tanner fell back to the bed and watched Justin get dressed. "I have today off. I'll be right here. Alright? If you need something, just let me know."

"Will you feed Butter Bunny?"

"Of course. I'll take care of our girl."

Justin's eyes shot to his, a stricken look on his face.

Tanner frowned. What had he said?

"I'll be back in a few hours." Justin walked away quickly, and Tanner heard the front door open and close.

Damn it. That hadn't gone horribly wrong, but it hadn't gone right either. He jumped out of bed and pulled his phone from his pocket. He had several texts and knew it hadn't taken until noon for the news to spread.

He texted Caden back.

Tanner: He just left the apartment. He wanted to be alone and process things. He said he's going to drive around.

Caden: I'm coming over. Grey will stay at his place just in case Justin goes there.

Tanner: He won't be back here for a while, Caden. He really wanted to go.

Caden: Shut up. You're my friend, and you loved her too. I know you did. Getting in the car now.

Tanner set the phone aside and closed his eyes. He let

the tears fall. He thought about lunches at the diner with Rhonda. They talked about Justin and his plans for the future. He had shown her the ring, and she had cried. He thought of all the times he picked her up from Dr. Woodward's office. She had seen the woman twice a week for five months. Tanner had paid for her sessions, so he knew she never missed an appointment.

Every time she left the office, she had been a quiet wreck. He would drive her around for a bit before taking her to Honey Buns for a coffee and a muffin. She had loved Zoe's banana nut muffins.

He knew Justin and she had had a strained relationship, but Justin always took care of her. He made sure her rent was paid and she had groceries in her fridge. Tanner's omega had loved his mom, even though she was far from perfect.

Tanner had loved the damn woman too.

"Tanner?" Caden let himself in the front door.

He wiped his face and met him in the living room. His friend just opened his arms.

Tanner didn't hesitate. He hugged the other alpha and cried.

Caden held him while Tanner grieved. After a while, Tanner's mind cleared and his tears slowed.

"Thanks, man. I'm sorry I got snot all over your shoulder."

Caden smiled sadly. "Worth it."

Butter Bunny hopped over and sat on Tanner's foot. "Are you ready for breakfast, B.B.?"

He dislodged the bunny and got the dry rabbit food from the cabinet next to the fridge. He rummaged around and grabbed a few baby carrots and a couple leafs of lettuce.

Butter Bunny's rabbit condo was in the living room, right

in front of one of the big windows. The rabbit hopped up her ramp and watched Tanner fill her bowl and set the veggies next to the water drip.

"Grey texted," Caden said. "Justin just pulled into his driveway."

Tanner let out a sigh of relief. "I wish he didn't pull away when he was hurting."

"Justin is a prickly bugger. I don't think he had anyone growing up. He's used to dealing with things on his own."

"He's not alone anymore. The look he gave me when he left wasn't promising." Tanner dropped into one of the large, overstuffed chairs. "I think he may leave me."

Caden sat on the ottoman nearby. "I think you're reading too much into it. Right now, he's feeling vulnerable. Give it some time before you panic."

Tanner dug the ring out of his pocket. He opened the small case and showed it to Caden. It was an Art Deco Tiffany & Co. vintage engagement ring. The diamond glittered in the sunlight streaming through the windows.

"Damn."

"It cost a little over five thousand. I'll have the loan paid off in two more months."

"It's beautiful, Tanner. When are you going to ask him?"

"I've just been waiting for the right moment." Tanner made a face. "With Rhonda's death, I'm afraid he'll push me further away. I wanted to be here for him, but he left. I wish I had asked him before now so he wouldn't think it was just because of his mom." He wiped his tears away. "I love him and want to spend the rest of my life with him."

"Then you definitely need to give it some time before you panic. I know Justin loves you. He has some fears and self-doubt to work through, and now with his mom's death, you need to have some patience. He'll get there." Caden grinned. "He'll love that ring too."

"David helped me pick it out." The retired beta was a sweet man with really good taste.

"The man knows his jewelry." Caden stood and patted his shoulder. "Get some sleep, Tanner. I'm going to go downstairs and see what I can do to help open the pub. It's already ten."

Tanner shook his head. "I'll help. I can't sleep right now."

If he couldn't hold Justin while he grieved, then Tanner would make sure Justin's beloved pub ran smoothly.

16
___

JUSTIN

Justin didn't realize he was at Grey's house until he put the car in park and got out. His head was a whirl of emotions and thoughts.

Caden, Grey, and Abel were Justin's best friends. When they met, all four of them were a mess, so they'd vowed to help each other turn things around. So far, they had done well by one another, but Justin hated needing help. He hated *needing* anyone.

His friend waited on the porch. Grey hugged the post and watched him with tear-filled eyes.

Grey's two dogs and miniature pig sat beside him, looking almost as concerned as their human.

"Justin." Grey pulled him into a hug as soon as Justin got to the top of the steps. "I'm so sorry."

Justin leaned into him, taking a deep breath of his familiar scent. He loved Grey so much. Before they had met, friends were something Justin never expected to have. He knew people around town and had a few acquaintances, but he hadn't known what friendship was until Grey and the others.

"Where is Auggie?" Grey's youngest was six months old, and he was Justin's favorite.

"He's taking a nap, but he'll be happy to give you some snuggles in another thirty minutes," Grey answered. "Come on in. Caden is keeping Tanner company, and Abel skyped me. He's waiting to see you too."

Justin felt guilt shoot through him. He hadn't thought anything about leaving Tanner. He hadn't thought about Tanner at all, only himself.

Grey gently shook him. "I know that look, Justin. There's nothing to feel guilty over. Come on. Let's see Abel."

Grey tugged him into the warm cabin. Grey's laptop sat on the coffee table, and they sat on the couch. Abel's worried face filled the screen. Palm trees and a beach hut were behind him. "Justin, sweetie. I'm so sorry."

"It's... I'm alright," Justin said, blinking away his tears. "I'm processing everything." He leaned his head against Grey's shoulder when the other man wrapped an arm around him. "Tell me about your vacation. Please."

Abel made a face. "Don't worry about that. I'm sorry I can't be there. I checked flights, but the earliest is tomorrow morning."

"No," Justin said, voice firm. "You will stay there for the rest of the week like you planned. Now, tell me about the beach."

"Justin."

"Tell him, Abel," Grey said softly.

Abel sighed. "Truthfully, it sucks. I miss home."

"Seriously?" Justin snorted. "You're on the beach, staying in a private, luxury resort, and you miss Maine? It's raining, Abel."

"I like the rain." Abel pouted. "Ernie is embarrassing too.

He just sits on the beach and knits. He knits. At the beach. Surrounded by hot men."

Ernie shoved his brother over, and his freckled face appeared on the screen. "Don't listen to him, Justin. He's the embarrassing one. Every night he insists on sampling each beer the bar or restaurant serves like he's at a wine tasting. He takes a sip and swishes it around his mouth before spitting it out and describing it." Ernie stroked his chin. "This one has a deep, mahogany taste with a touch of coconut."

Justin and Grey laughed, bodies shaking against one another.

"I never said that," Abel said, trying to shove his brother out of the screen.

"A few days ago, he spit beer all over the server, then told him that it tasted worse than swill."

"It was disgusting." Abel made a face.

The brothers finally settled on squishing together so Justin could see them both.

"I had to apologize for you. *That* was embarrassing." Ernie's face turned sly. "Last night, he met an alpha. The man is a bartender here at the resort."

"Abel." Justin gasped, sadness lightening for a moment. As playful and wild as Abel was, he seldom dated, and he *never* did one-night stands.

"Tell us." Grey's eyes danced as he clapped his hands.

Abel groaned. "Really, Ernie? Did you have to tell them?"

"Yes." Ernie nodded, face serious. "He didn't come back to our hut until this morning. It was his first walk of shame."

"I don't even know his last name." Abel covered his face with his hands. "He is so hot though. Big and muscly." He looked up, eyes all dreamy. "So yummy."

"I can't believe it." Justin shook his head.

"I couldn't resist him. His smile melted me into a puddle of goo." Abel shrugged and grinned.

They laughed at Abel and teased him a little longer.

Justin smiled softly. This was what he needed. A break and a bit of silliness.

"Justin, we're coming back tomorrow." Ernie brushed a strand of his red hair from his face, his eyes sympathetic.

"I'll be alright." Justin leaned on Grey again. "I'm just so mad at her right now. God, it hurts so much, but at the same time, I just want to smack her."

"I don't blame you," Grey said. "It's okay to be mad and miss her both."

"She made a bad decision." Abel sniffled and wiped his eyes. "That doesn't mean you have to stop loving her. It doesn't mean you don't get to mourn her."

"I think Tanner is going to leave me." Justin bit his lip and watched his friends' reactions.

"Huh?" Ernie exchanged a puzzled look with Abel. "Where did that come from?"

"He puts up with so much from me, but this is too much. Who wants a broken-hearted omega?"

"If that omega is you, then Tanner does," Grey said bluntly.

"I'm pregnant," Justin said bluntly.

"Holy shit," Abel said. "I leave for one week, and your life goes crazy dramatic!"

"What did Tanner say?" Grey kissed the top of Justin's head.

"I haven't told him. He's going to leave me. He *has* to leave me if he wants to get anywhere in his career. This town won't elect a sheriff that's hooked to me."

"Okay. Hold on." Ernie frowned. "Does Tanner want to

be sheriff? Sheriff McKenzie isn't planning on retiring for a while."

"He hasn't said," Justin admitted. "It's the natural progression for his career though."

"Stop." Abel shook the screen. "You need to just still your mind for a minute. Justin, you're pregnant, and your mom just passed away. Don't fill your head with reasons to run from the one person you want the most just because you're upset and afraid."

Justin's mouth dropped open. Damn, was he doing that?

"He's right." Grey hugged him close. "You've had one foot out the door since you started dating Tanner. Right now, your world is changing, and you're scared. Don't make a decision you'll regret."

"Give Tanner the benefit of the doubt." Abel smiled softly. "That man adores you, and you should let him make his own decisions."

"I'm not good enough for him."

"If you don't want him, I would be happy to take Tanner off your hands." Ernie tilted his head and eyed Justin through the screen.

"Back the fuck off, red!" Justin's words surprised him. The pain at the thought of Tanner with someone else was excruciating. "Oh. Damn it."

"It's too late to back out, isn't it?" Ernie grinned. "You love him, and you're not going to let him go, are you?"

"No." Justin shook his head.

"Then there's no sense in even contemplating leaving him." Abel nodded and fist bumped Ernie.

"What if he leaves me? I'm really not good enough for him."

"Justin, do you think Yeo is good enough for Caden?" Grey asked.

"Yeah. They fit perfectly."

"Yeo's dad is a monster. He tried to kill Yeo's papa."

Justin swallowed, thinking about Yeo's papa, Dean. "Yeo isn't like his father. He's a lot better than him."

Grey framed Justin's face in his hands. "Then why should your mom's addiction define you?"

"I... I don't know."

"Are you ashamed of her?" Abel's tone was gentle, but his words cut Justin to the bone.

As much as he hated the drugs, he didn't hate his mom. On one hand, she was neglectful and selfish when she was high. On the other hand, when she was sober, she was kind to others and always thought the best of people. He always wished he was more like that.

"I am," Justin answered in a small voice.

"I know she hurt you with her carelessness." Grey hugged him again. "Would you do that to your child? Would you ignore them, forget to feed them?"

"Never." Justin laid a hand across his flat abdomen. He would be there for his baby.

"Your persistence, intelligence, and kindness is what defines you." Abel grinned. "Though the kindness part is still kind of new."

Justin snorted. "That's the truth. You have no idea how hard it is to not hate you all."

Grey cleared his throat and glared at Justin. "The point here is that you are your own person. Your mom will always be a part of your past. Her behavior helped shape you, but it does *not* make you who you are."

"Maybe you're right. Maybe I'm just making excuses." Justin shrugged. He would need to think on this.

"We are right," Abel said. "So, problem one is solved.

You will stay with Tanner and trust him to make his own decisions."

Ernie nodded. "If you don't, I'm taking him. Keep that in mind, Mr. Ames."

Justin stuck his tongue out at Ernie. Tanner was his, damn it.

"Problem two might take some time," Grey said. "I don't know how to make this better, Justin. When my parents and brother died, I just shut down. It took time and meeting you guys to get to a place where I could deal with it."

Justin shoved his face into Grey's shoulder. How could he miss her so much already? How could he miss her and be so angry at her at the same time?

"What we can do is be there for you." Abel sniffed and hugged Ernie. "We're coming back tomorrow. That's that."

"I miss my alpacas and sheep, so it's not just for you." Ernie gave him a stubborn look. Justin had a feeling they would be home soon whether he liked it or not.

"Caden is taking care of the pub, and I'll help you with funeral arrangements." Grey stroked Justin's back. "You aren't alone."

Justin smiled into Grey's shoulder. He really wasn't alone anymore. He never really had his mom, but he had his best friends. He had Tanner.

The front door swung open, startling Grey and Justin. Together, they watched Harper run in, Rue perched on his hip. Harper and Grey's son was a pudgy and adorable toddler. Grey's alpha was adorable in a whole other way.

"I held them back as long as I could, sunshine," Harper panted. "I'm sorry, Justin. They're coming."

"Get out of my way," Grammy said, pushing Harper out of the doorway. "Where's Justin?"

"Mi corazón, where is your best friend? Where is Justin?" Ines was right behind Grammy.

The two women saw him at the same time and rushed over, shoving Grey aside so they could hug Justin. Before he knew what was happening, he was wrapped in their arms, crying.

Grammy's soft arms held him tightly while Ines stroked his back and whispered soft words of comfort. He vaguely heard Grey and Harper talking.

"Gramps and a few others went to help out at the pub," Harper said. "Grammy sent someone to talk to the sheriff now. We'll head to the funeral home soon to make the arrangements. Justin won't have to worry about anything."

"Abel and Ernie are flying home in the morning." Grey hugged his alpha. "We'll be here for him. Everyone will be."

GRAMMY INSISTED on driving Justin home when he decided he was ready to go. Her calm presence and the comfortable silence was a balm for the painful day.

Grey and his family were arranging the funeral. It would be in three days. Justin was relieved not to have to deal with all the details. It was going to be hard enough to just get through it all. He had never relied on others as easily as he was relying on the Wilson family. Justin felt a little guilty, but mostly, he just wanted Tanner's arms around him.

Abel and Ernie would be home tomorrow night. Justin had tried to talk the men into finishing their vacation, but they had insisted they needed to be here.

Grammy drove the car behind the pub and parked in Justin's usual spot. Ines parked her own car next to them.

"Thank you, Grammy."

The woman gave him a watery smile. "I can only imagine what you're feeling right now, Justin."

"I'm so mad at her."

"Rhonda did a stupid thing, and it cost her the rest of her life." Grammy took his hand. "That doesn't mean she didn't love you, Justin. She tried so hard. Ines and I spent a lot of time with her, and she talked about you all the time. She was so proud of you."

"Tanner helped her too. Mom was seeing a therapist. Did you know?"

Grammy looked surprised. "I didn't. She was always so quiet when we visited, but she would smile and laugh with us."

"I think, if she had had more time... But she doesn't. She's gone." Justin felt something break inside him.

She was gone. She would never get better. He would never develop the relationship he wanted with her. It was done. All he would ever have of her were a few good memories.

Tanner opened the car door and knelt beside him. The rain pelted his alpha, but his big body blocked Justin from getting wet.

"Hey, honey."

Justin unbuckled his seatbelt and pushed into Tanner's arms. He wrapped his arms around Tanner's neck and buried his face against his chest.

"Whoa." Tanner fell back, landing in a puddle.

He held Justin tightly, settling him on his lap.

"Don't worry, boys," Grammy said. She and Ines held umbrellas over them. "Ines and I have you."

"I'm so sorry I left you, Tanner. I didn't think about how you must be feeling."

"I'm alright, honey. You needed to clear your head. I get it."

"Tanner, I love you."

"I love you too. Let's go inside where it's dry." Tanner tried to get up, but Justin refused to move.

"I don't want you to leave. Not ever. Even if it means you can't be sheriff."

"Huh?" Tanner's hand tilted Justin's face up. "Sheriff? I don't want to be sheriff. I'm confused."

"I want you to move in with me. You've asked before, but I was stupid. I want you with me." Justin's voice cracked. "I'm all in, Tanner – both feet in the door."

"I don't understand, but I'm sure as hell going to say yes." Tanner gave him a gentle kiss. "I love you, Justin. I've wanted this for a long time, but are you sure? Is this some reaction to losing Rhonda?"

"It's not a reaction." Justin wiped his eyes. "It's a realization. I don't want to waste any time with you."

Tanner kissed him, lips soft and warm against Justin's.

"We'll help him move his things." Ines smiled down at them. "You boys have more important things to focus on."

Justin shot her a soft smile, then kissed Tanner again. They sat in the rain, with two chattering women standing over them. Justin felt a little less empty with every kiss.

17

———

TANNER

It took a while and several kisses, but Tanner finally convinced Justin to lay down. He tucked the blankets around his omega, then checked on Butter Bunny. He gave the bunny her dinner, then jumped into the shower, letting the hot water ease his aches and pains. He wanted to go downstairs and make sure the pub was running smoothly.

He dried off and grabbed his toothbrush. Halfway through brushing his teeth, his hand froze. His eyes were glued on the garbage can and the white stick poking out.

Tanner's hands shook as he picked it up and looked at the two pink lines. "Oh, fuck."

Butter Bunny hopped through the open door and sat on his foot. Tanner picked her up and held her tightly to his bare chest.

"B.B., we're having a baby. Holy fuck."

Wait. Why hadn't Justin told him? Tanner's eyes filled as he answered his own question. Justin hadn't told him because his mom just died. On top of that, it looked like he'd just found out, and he apparently had a lot of self-doubt. Tanner thought about Justin's words from earlier. He obviously thought Tanner's career suffered because they were together.

"Prickly idiot." Tanner wiped a hand across his face, then dropped a kiss on top of Butter Bunny's head. "I love him, B.B., but he can be stubborn. I don't want to be sheriff, but even if I did, my relationship with Justin wouldn't get in the way."

He set the rabbit down, then finished dressing.

The rain was pelting the porch roof when he left the apartment. He took a minute to breath, fighting a grin. A baby. They were having a baby. How could he want to cry and laugh at the same time? His stomach churned with grief and joy. Damn, he wished Rhonda was there.

He sighed and walked down the stairs to the pub.

The kitchen was busy when he walked in. At least twenty orders were on the screen and Albie was rushing to fill them. Grey and his father-in-law, Bennett, were pitching in. Bennett worked at the cutting board, and Grey plated the food.

"Fuck. It's late. Doesn't the kitchen close in thirty minutes?"

"We'll stay open until the orders stop pouring in." Albie looked unconcerned. "The place is packed."

"Is he resting?" Bennett looked up from chopping potatoes for the pub's specialty – loaded pub fries.

"Finally. Thought I'd check in for him and see if it was as busy as it was at lunch."

"It's been crazy all evening." Albie flipped a pile of shredded steak, then turned and took a sheet out of the oven. It was full of large ramekins filled with the pub's Guinness, beef, and mushroom shepherd's pie.

Tanner's mouth watered. That was one of his favorite

dishes. He wasn't even hungry, but he wanted to devour the twenty servings laid out on the counter.

"That big guy, Reuben, stayed late to help out," Grey said. "He just left a few minutes ago."

"All the busy bodies in town want to gossip about Rhonda," Bennett growled.

"Don't let it get to you," Albie said. "Justin will make a lot of money tonight, and the fuckers won't get a peek at him."

Tanner smiled softly. Justin had a good crew here. "You all need any help?"

"We got this." Albie shot a grin over his shoulder. "I imagine the servers could use a hand though."

Tanner nodded, then left the kitchen. "Damn." Every table and barstool in the place was taken.

"Tanner." Gramps stood behind the bar, pulling drafts of beer. "Can you check on tables? Those poor servers are getting overwhelmed."

Gramps, Caden, and Wiley tended the bar and Tanner could see four of Justin's servers running around the room. Fortunately, it looked like a few more Wilsons had decided to pitch in by serving tables. Otherwise, the evening servers may have revolted.

"Hey." Travis popped up. "Need some help here?"

"Hell, yes." Tanner handed him a tray. "Start bussing tables, hot shot."

Travis patted his shoulder. "You got it."

Tanner grabbed a tray and carried a drink order to one of the tables. From there, he carried dishes to the kitchen, refilled drinks, and bussed tables.

They were half way through the night when Chelsea walked in. Wiley had mentioned she'd been fired, so Tanner didn't suppose she was there for anything good.

Chelsea pushed through the crowd to the bar. "Where's Justin?"

"Resting upstairs. What do you want?" Tanner crossed his arms over his chest and glared at the woman.

Laura and North came to stand next to him, echoing his stance.

"Aww, does Mr. Stuck Up miss his mommy?" Chelsea turned to her friends and laughed. "I told you guys that Justin was just like us. His trashy ass mom just proved it. Stupid bitch didn't even have that much. Wally said he only gave her three percs. We all had that many this morning."

"You bitch!" Laura launched himself at the woman, but Tanner caught her in his arms before she could touch Chelsea.

Chelsea laughed. "I'm just telling it like it is."

She kept laughing until Sheriff McKenzie grabbed her arm. "Ma'am, you just admitted to illegal use of prescription medication. We'll be taking you and your friends here down to the station for a drug test."

Tanner and Travis corralled Chelsea's three friends.

"This is harassment." Chelsea's voice went high. "I'm just here to get some things I left."

"You literally just said, in front of multiple witnesses, that you had already taken at least three Percocet." Travis looked at her in disbelief. "I don't imagine you have a prescription."

"You're horrible woman." An older lady from Rhonda's trailer park tsked. "Rhonda was a sweetheart. She wasn't a bit indecent, even with her problems. How dare you call her trashy? How dare you compare yourself to her?"

Another of Rhonda's neighbors crossed her arms and glared at Chelsea. "She surely wouldn't be so cruel to another person. You came here to hurt Justin. Talk about trashy!"

Sheriff McKenzie snorted. "Agreed."

They marched the four people out of the pub, and Tanner helped the sheriff get them situated in two patrol cars.

"I'm sorry about all this, Tanner. I'm glad Justin wasn't here." Sherriff McKenzie opened his door. "I've been wanting dirt on Wally for a while, and these idiots may lead me there. Travis is going to check and see if she really left anything here. I have an idea of why she really came in tonight."

Tanner waited until the sheriff drove away. He ran his hands over his head and did his best to get rid of the anger.

"I wanted to hit her." Laura came to stand beside him, trembling with fury.

"Justin needs you here, not in jail. I know it would have been satisfying, but that wouldn't be a smart thing to do in front of everyone."

"We'll save that shit for our next night out," North said, snarling toward the door. "Can you believe her?"

"We could *accidently* shave her head." Grey looked thoughtful. "That would last longer than a beat down."

"Let Sheriff McKenzie handle it, guys. He's been wanting to get to Wally for a while. Everyone knows where the drugs are but pinning him down is the problem."

"Have it your way." Laura stomped her foot.

"She'll get what's coming to her. Karma can be a bitch." Caden smiled. "I may offer my services to the sheriff."

Tanner grinned. "Get back to work, guys. We have a pub to run."

Before he knew it, closing time had long since passed.

He turned the open sign off and locked the door before turning around and groaning.

Tanner gave North a look of sympathy. "Damn, my feet hurt. How the hell do you all do this all the time?"

"You get used to it, man." The young alpha looked exhausted. "Laura and I both worked a double today. We're glad Chelsea is gone, but damn, the timing sucks."

"Good riddance to the bitch." Laura groaned as she settled onto one of the stools to count her tips.

One by one, the pub's employees finished up and clocked out.

Albie was the last to go. "I'll come in around twelve tomorrow. It will probably be busy again."

"That's in seven hours, Albie. You need sleep."

"Don't doubt my staying power, Tanner." Albie mock growled.

Tanner laughed. "Okay. Okay."

Gramps patted him on the back. "I'm heading out too. I'll get someone in tomorrow to tend the bar. Wiley needs a good night's rest, since he worked all day."

"Thanks, Gramps. We really appreciate you all helping out."

"Ever since Grey and Justin became friends, we've seen Justin as ours. You too, Tanner. If you need anything, make sure to let us know."

"We will."

An hour later, Tanner drug himself up the stairs. It was still raining, and he sat in one of the deck chairs. The sound of the rain soothed him, and he was asleep in seconds.

"Tanner." Justin sounded amused.

Tanner's eyes popped open. Daylight filtered through the rain and highlighted the white streaks in Justin's blond hair.

Justin held Butter Bunny in his arms and smiled down at Tanner. "How long have you been sleeping out here?"

"Since six." He rolled his shoulders and popped his neck. "You made a lot of money last night. The pub didn't close until around five."

"Oh, no. We're short a server and bartender. I should have…"

"We took care of it. The Wilsons jumped in to help, and you have an awesome crew, love." Tanner pulled Justin onto his lap and set Butter Bunny down. "I knew you worked hard, but I never appreciated how hard."

Justin cupped his face. "Thank you for helping last night. I haven't thought of the pub since you told me about Mom."

Tanner leaned forward and kissed Justin. His tongue slid in, and the kiss deepened.

Justin groaned and pressed his ass against Tanner's erection. "Can't have sex on my porch."

Tanner stood, holding Justin in his arms. "That can be fixed."

He carried him to the door, and Justin pushed it open. Butter Bunny hopped through, and Tanner followed her in.

Reaching the bedroom, he gently laid Justin on the bed. He laughed when his omega grabbed his shirt and pulled him down on top of him. Their bodies settled against each other, fitting together perfectly.

"I hate it when you're not here." Justin pressed kisses to his face. "I hate sleeping alone. I hate cooking and eating alone. I miss cuddling with you and Butter Bunny and watching that stupid show you like."

"*The Walking Dead* is not stupid."

Justin kissed him and wrapped his legs around Tanner's waist, pressing their dicks together. "I hate zombies."

Tanner hummed and pressed against Justin. "Less clothes. We need less clothes."

Justin had Tanner's pants off in seconds. His warm mouth wrapped around Tanner's dick, and he groaned. Justin cupped Tanner's balls and licked and sucked his hard dick. Tanner clutched Justin's head and arched his hips, sinking deeper into his mouth.

A few minutes later, Justin's mouth moved slowly off Tanner's dick while twirling his tongue around the head. His omega licked up and down Tanner's shaft slowly while caressing his balls. "I love the way you taste."

"I want in you," Tanner growled, pulling at Justin's clothes.

He had Justin naked and stretched quickly. Tanner paused as he reached for a condom, then left it on the bed stand. He made a mental note to talk to Justin about that.

He pushed into the omega, enjoying the smooth heat as Justin's body clenched around Tanner's dick. His speed picked up, and soon, he was pounding into his omega, Justin meeting his pace.

He reached between them and stroked Justin's dick, relishing the sounds his man made. Justin screamed as he came, shooting all over Tanner's hand. He licked his hand clean, then focused on Justin's ass. He leaned down and kissed Justin, loving the closeness and intimacy of the moment.

How had he ever lived without Justin?

Tanner didn't last much longer. He came, filling Justin's body and moaning into his omega's mouth. He rolled to the side, and they lay together, breathing heavily. Justin settled his head on Tanner's shoulder and wrapped an arm around his waist.

"You weren't wearing underwear."

"Nope." Justin nuzzled against his neck. "I had hopes."

Tanner laughed. "I'm always yours, honey." He leaned down and kissed his omega's head. "There was something I needed to talk to you about though."

"Uh oh. That doesn't sound good."

"There's nothing to worry about. Zero percentage of worry needed."

Justin laughed. "Okay then."

"I saw your pregnancy test in the bathroom trash can."

Justin sat up quickly. "Oh, fuck."

Tanner leaned up and pulled Justin back into his arms. "Zero worries, honey."

Justin leaned his head back on Tanner's chest and groaned. "Fuck."

"It's like everything decided to go nuts at once, isn't it?"

Justin nodded. "Yeah. I planned on telling you once I wrapped my mind around it."

"I love the idea of having a baby with you, Justin." Tanner tilted his omega's face up. "Is that why you want me to move in? If it is, I completely understand."

Justin's green eyes softened. "No, you big dumbass. With everything going on and after talking to the guys, I realized I can't give you up. It would be better for you if I did, but I can't."

"Is it because you feel alone now that Rhonda is gone?"

"No. Absolutely not. I've been thinking about it for a while, and I'm lonely without you here. I want you here. I'll fucking fight for you, Tanner, and for us. I can totally take Ernie out. He's a teacher and I own a pub, so no problems there."

Tanner tried not to laugh, but he couldn't help it. "I don't know. Ernie has those knitting needles. I'm picturing this as an epic battle in an old, black-and-white Kung Fu movie."

Justin laughed. "More like *Kung Fu Panda*."

Tanner smiled and swung an arm over the side of the bed, digging around in the pocket of his jeans. "Just so you know, I bought this four months ago. There's absolutely no pressure, but I wanted you to know this is where we're going."

He set the ring box on his stomach and opened it.

Justin's eyes widened, and he sat up again. "Oh, my god."

Tanner watched Justin. "I bought it before I found out about the baby and before you asked me to move in. I love you, Justin Ames."

"Tanner." Justin's eyes filled with tears.

"I remember the day we met. I was kicking myself for never making a move on Elijah Wilson, and for being an asshole to him in high school." Tanner smirked.

"Fucking Wilsons get all the attention." Justin snorted. "I had wanted you for ages, but did you notice me? No."

"Then suddenly there was this adorably hot, blond angel right there in front of me. I knew you were mine from the moment I really saw you. I knew that everything in my life was leading straight to you."

"I'm not perfect." Justin sighed. "I'm a prickly, moody bastard with baggage and pettiness and a whole host of other ugly qualities."

"You're a good man." Tanner glared at Justin. Why Justin couldn't see the amazing person he was completely baffled Tanner.

"I guess I'm alright." Justin shrugged.

"You work so hard at everything you do, whether it's the pub or helping the Wilsons with their farm. You're kind and fair to your employees. Each of them adore you and Abel."

"They're good workers, so I don't have to bring out my mean too often."

Tanner reached out and held Justin's hand, then kissed his omega's palm. "You're a good friend and a wonderful boyfriend. You love me, even when I make you watch *The Walking Dead*."

"It's hard sometimes. The whiny humans need to just focus on killing walkers. Damn."

Tanner grinned. "You and I are meant to be, love. That's just how it is."

Justin picked up the ring box and stared at it for a while. "Okay."

"Okay? You'll marry me?" Tanner sat up. "Seriously?"

"Both feet in, right?" Justin's voice was shaky. "I'm scared, Tanner. I'm so afraid you'll realize what a mistake you're making."

"You and I aren't a mistake." Tanner closed his eyes for a moment, struggling to find a way to make Justin see. "You remember the ballgame we went to? Police versus fire fighters?"

"Which one?"

"The last one?"

Justin looked confused. "I remember. You got ribbed from your buddies on both teams."

"All night, the guys kept telling me they were going to steal you away from me. Fuck, Sheriff McKenzie told me you were too good for a jackass like me."

"Really? He said that?"

"Yeah." Tanner cupped Justin's face. "It's not just me. Everyone thinks we belong together. That a jackass like me deserves someone as wonderful as you. Yes, the whole town knows our business. They know what you went through as a kid and what a jerk I was as a teenager, but that's in the past, and the only people that matter care about who we are now. The people that matter want to see us happy together. I want to be with you forever."

Justin kissed Tanner and watched him with sad eyes. "I love you and want us to be happy. That's all. After Mom's funeral. After we say goodbye to her... I don't want to wait to get married. People may talk about us, but I want to be yours now. Mom would want us to be together too." Justin took a deep breath. "Let's go to Vegas. I don't want a big thing. I just want it to be us. Our day. Can it be just you and me? Will your family care?"

"They'll understand. They're in California now anyway." Tanner felt excitement burn a path through his veins. They were doing this. Holy shit.

"They don't like me anyway."

Tanner winced. His parents weren't happy with Tanner's choice, but they lived across the country and saw him maybe once a year. It wasn't their business.

"Their opinion doesn't matter. I love you, and we have plenty of friends and family here."

"Alright. We'll get through the funeral, and I'll deal with Mom's things. Then we get married."

"Sounds like a plan."

"Fuck. I need a new bartender."

18

JUSTIN

The next day, Justin, Grammy, and Ines sorted through his mom's trailer. Even though the place was clean and neat, there was so much stuff.

"This is pretty." Grammy held up a pink silk dress.

Justin remembered buying it for his mom a few months ago. She had loved it. "Is pink too bright for a funeral?"

"Sweetie, if you want her to wear it, then that's what she'll wear."

"She really liked it." Justin wiped his eyes. "It's just from Kohl's, but it's been years since she had a brand new dress."

"Then this is what she'll wear. I'll look for some shoes."

"There should be a pair of new heels in her closet."

"I'll find them." Grammy patted his cheek and went back into the bedroom.

"Justin?" Ines sounded uncertain. She was working on the second bedroom while Grammy went through his mom's clothes.

"Yeah?" He sniffed and wiped his eyes again. This shouldn't be so damn hard.

Ines held out a wrapped box. The wrapping paper was

purple with balloons all over it.

Justin closed his eyes. "My birthday is next week. I can't believe I forgot."

"Do you want to open it? You don't have to, cariño."

Justin took it and held the box in his hands. His mom's memory of birthdays and holidays was erratic at the best of times. He only remembered getting three birthday presents from her his whole life.

He took a breath and gently unwrapped the gift. A card sat atop a dark box. Liz Ross and David Westby were written in gold on the top, but he didn't recognize the name. He set the card aside and lifted the lid. He gasped, covering his mouth. Inside were four exquisite snow globes. Each had a solid, dark wood base, and there was one for each season of the year. The spring snow globe had a cherry blossom tree within it.

He picked it up and shook it. Pink petals filled the globe. "She's never... I've never gotten something this beautiful before."

"They are lovely." Ines sat beside him and wrapped an arm around his shoulders.

Justin set the snow globe back into the box and opened the card. Inside, his mom had written a note.

Justin,

Today celebrates a very special day! It was the greatest day of my life – the day you were born. I know we have our problems, but I will never stop loving you. I am so proud of the man you've become despite what I've put you through. You are so brave and so smart. I wish I had a quarter of your strength and will power. I wish I were worthy of being your mother.

I know I haven't given you much, but I hope this year will be different. I hope you enjoy your gift. I wanted to get you something you could use all the time, and with each change of the season, you can take one of these snow globes out and then I'm right there with you. I love you, son.

Happy Birthday! – Mom

Justin laid his head on the table and cried. Ines hugged him and murmured in Spanish.

His mom's words kept running through his mind. She hadn't thought she was worthy of being his mother.

"She was worthy." Justin's voice cracked. "I love her, Abuela. I love her even if she was selfish and took pills, even though she was never able to keep a job and never bought groceries. I love her even though the electricity and water were turned off all the time and my clothes were never new and always dirty. I love her even if she never asked me about school or about how I felt." He leaned into Ines and cried. "She was worthy. With all her flaws, she was worthy, because she loved me. I can't not love her. I've tried, fuck, I've tried. She made so many bad decisions. She was *my* mom though. Mine. I love her."

Justin thought about Tanner. Justin did his best by Tanner, and that made Justin worthy. He loved his alpha more than anything, and that made Justin worthy. He was a good person. He had learned from his past and always tried to be better, and that made Justin worthy.

He was worthy. He really was.

"I need to talk to Tanner." Justin rubbed his face and looked around. "He was right. I'm an idiot."

"You aren't an idiot." Grammy put her hands on his shoulders. Justin hadn't heard her come in. "You just needed to figure some things out. I take it you understand that your mom loved you, and she was trying to be stronger?"

"Yeah." Justin leaned into Ines. "I love her, and I wish I could have had more time with her. I hardly ever told her that. I hardly ever let myself think it."

"Oh, sweetie." Grammy stroked her fingers through his hair.

"I tell Tanner I love him every day, and I do love him." He laid a hand on his abdomen. "I will make sure our baby knows we love them. Every single day."

"Baby?" Grammy and Ines shared a startled look.

"You've been carrying some burdens, haven't you?" Ines kissed his cheek.

"We're going to be alright." Justin looked at his snow globes and grinned. "Tanner and I will be good daddies."

"We noticed that ring there." Grammy pointed at his engagement ring. "We were trying not to be nosy, but that looks like a lovely engagement ring."

"We're going to Las Vegas next week. I still need to run it by Abel, but that's our plan."

Ines cringed and held her hands to her chest. "I'm trying so hard not to beg you to have a big wedding. I. Will. Restrain. Myself."

Justin laughed. "Good job, Abuela."

Tanner stood beside him, holding his hand. Grey, Abel, and Caden stood on his other side, and Grammy and Ines stood behind him. The spring rain hadn't let up, and it seemed suitable for a burial.

The funeral service had been taken care of. Grammy's daughter, Anna, had arranged everything. All Justin had to do was pick out his mom's clothes and show up.

Most of the town had come. One of the local pastors gave a eulogy. Then they stuck her in the ground. Done.

"Are you alright?" Tanner squeezed Justin's hand.

Justin didn't know how he felt. He was mostly numb. "I

will be. *We* will be."

"Are you up for the wake? If not, we'll handle it." Grey wrapped an arm around Justin's waist.

"Will Auggie be there?" Justin badly wanted some snuggle time.

Grey snorted. "Yes, he'll be there."

"Okay." Justin gave Tanner a nod, and they headed to the car.

Once they were on the road, Justin grabbed Tanner's hand again. "How are you doing?"

Tanner looked sad. "I keep thinking about the baby and how Rhonda would have been so excited. We had plans for your birthday next week. It just doesn't seem real."

"I know what you mean."

Abel had insisted they close The Irish Rose for the day, so they could have the wake there. Justin couldn't argue too much. It was right beneath his house.

Tanner and Justin went in through the kitchen. Albie and Reuben were putting the finishing touches on the food, and Grey waited with Auggie.

"There's my handsome boy." Justin held his arms out.

"I'm watching you, August Wilson." Tanner mock glared at the baby.

Auggie just giggled and ignored him.

Justin held the baby close and breathed in his sweet baby scent. Auggie settled his head on Justin's chest, holding tight to his favorite blankie.

Justin turned to his cooks. "Thank you, guys. You didn't have to do all of this."

The men had made a ton of comfort food and large portions of most of the pub's signature dishes.

"It was no problem," Albie said. "I'm helping to eat it all anyway."

Reuben just grunted. He tilted his head to the door, and Justin followed him. He knew Reuben wouldn't be staying. The man couldn't deal with all these people in his kitchen.

"Friend's moving up in two weeks."

Justin's eyes widened. "The bartender?"

Reuben nodded. "Has a couple kids too."

"I'll start looking around for a rental for them." Justin was so relieved. If Reuben recommended the guy, Justin knew he'd be a keeper.

Reuben's dark skin flushed. "Mr. Wilson already did."

Justin snorted and stroked Auggie's back. "Gramps knows everything."

The kitchen door opened and Wilsons poured in, Gramps in the lead.

"Boys, get the food out to the buffet table," Gramps said, snapping his fingers at his children and grandchildren.

They all moved fast to obey him. Justin laughed at them as Gramps started sorting everyone and assigning them tasks.

Tanner shared a look with him from across the kitchen. Justin's alpha was already eating a small bowl of the pub's Guinness, beef, and mushroom shepherd's pie. He turned back to Reuben, then blinked, confused. His cook stood frozen in place, eyes fixed on Ernie. A look of longing covered his broad face, making Justin's heart hurt.

Reuben shook his head, then hugged Justin and Auggie. "Sorry about your mom."

The big man slipped out the door before more people could invade his kitchen. Justin watched him go, completely baffled.

"Was that your cook, Reuben?" Grammy was suddenly at his side.

"Uh, yeah." Justin shook his head. "He doesn't do well

around a lot of people. He's a sweetheart, though."

"Hmm." The spark in Grammy's eyes didn't bode well for poor Reuben.

"Don't scare him off, Grammy." Abel hugged Justin and Auggie. "He's the third best thing to happen to the pub."

"The third?"

"You're the first best thing, and obviously, I'm the next best thing."

"You are so modest." Justin rolled his eyes, then frowned. "Will you be alright while Tanner and I are gone?"

"Absolutely." Abel smiled confidently. "I'm pulling in a few family members to help out until you're home and we get our new bartender."

Abel's smile faltered, and it was Justin's turn to hug his friend. "You miss your guy, don't you?"

"He was so sweet." Abel's eyes watered. "It wasn't a one-night stand. Not for me."

"Did you tell him you had to leave early?"

"I couldn't find him. I left a message at the bar, but what if he didn't find it?" Abel wiped his eyes. "It doesn't matter. What matters is that I'm here for you. Are you okay?"

"I don't know. I don't want to go out there."

"You can stay in here as long as you want." Grammy patted his cheek.

"No. Everyone came to say goodbye to Mom."

Tanner finally reached him and pulled him into his arms. "Do you feel up to socializing?"

"I think so. We can make the rounds, then eat some of this good food." He handed Auggie to Grammy, wishing he could keep the baby with him.

They started around the room. So many people were there, and they all wanted to give Justin their condolences.

"We'll take it one person at a time," Tanner whispered in

his ear.

They started working their way through the room of people.

"I'm so sorry for your loss."

"She was a good woman. You have my condolences."

"If you need anything, please let us know. You're in our thoughts and prayers."

After a while, everything ran together. *Everyone* ran together.

"Uh, hi." The man in front of him looked like he was about to puke. The omega was slight, with tan skin and dark hair, and he had a toddler perched on his hip. Justin didn't recognize him at all.

Justin shrugged. He thought he knew everyone in town, but apparently not. "Hi? I guess?"

His dark eyes followed Justin's every move. "You're Justin."

"Yes, I am." Justin shared a look with Tanner. This was weird.

"My name is Griff."

"It's nice to meet you. Did you know my mother?"

"No. We knew about her though. When we heard she died, I wanted to come, but this was probably a bad idea."

"What do you mean?"

"My name is Griff Ames. My dad's name is Joshua Ames."

Justin paled. *His* dad's name was Josh.

Griff looked defeated. "I didn't want to cause a scene or anything. I'm sorry. I just wanted to let you know we were sorry about her passing and that you're not alone."

Justin's heart beat fast, and he felt faint.

"Have an Auggie." Grey handed Justin his son, and Justin slowly calmed.

"Damn it, Grey." He couldn't be upset with his snuggle buddy in his arms.

"I really am sorry." Griff started to turn away. Justin didn't want that. This guy was his half-brother. Now that he knew to look for it, he could see his dad in the other man's features.

"Wait." Justin reached out and tugged on the toddler's foot. "Who's this little girl?"

"This is my daughter, Bea." Griff nibbled his lip. "You have another brother too, but he's overseas. Zed is in the marines. He really wanted to be here and told me to tell you he was sorry."

"Oh god." Justin swallowed hard. "This is crazy. What about Dad?"

"We knew he was married before and had another kid, but he never really talked about you guys. He left my mom too. I was six and Zed was ten."

"That's not surprising." Justin tugged Bea's foot again and smiled when she giggled. "Maybe... Maybe we can talk sometime."

"Here's my number." Griff handed him a card. "Anytime, just give me a call. I can get you Zed's e-mail also. He would love to hear from you."

"Thanks. It might be a while, but I'll give you a call." Justin watched his brother leave.

"So much drama." Abel watched Justin in awe.

"Seriously." Grey shook his head, dazed.

They moved on to the next person, but Justin was out of it. All he could think about was his mom's broken heart and his new siblings.

Justin kissed Auggie's head and leaned into Tanner. His mom was gone, but he had Tanner and his friends. He would be strong and see this through. For her.

19

TANNER

Two weeks later, Tanner put the car in park. "We're home, honey. Finally."

Justin stretched in his seat and smiled wide. Two weeks of sun and sex had been just what they both needed. His omega was tan, well-rested, and relaxed. After his mom's death, the surprise visit from Griff, and the quick marriage, Justin had needed the break. Hell, Tanner had too.

"Home." Justin hummed happily. "I missed Butter Bunny. I even missed those damn Wilsons."

"That's good, because two of them are headed this way." Tanner pointed out the window.

Grey and Abel ran toward the car and opened Justin's door, pulling him out. They hugged each other and squealed over the wedding band nestled against Justin's engagement ring.

"Oh, hi guys. I'm home too." Tanner was completely ignored.

"I absolutely love that ring." Abel started tugging Justin toward the pub.

"You look so happy." Grey sniffled and wiped his eyes. "The vacation was just what you needed."

"It was wonderful. I had Tanner and lots of time to think." Justin's eyes twinkled. "I even won some money."

Abel and Grey squealed again. "How much? How much?"

"Five dollars." Justin smirked, then dug around in his pocket. He waved the five-dollar bill around. "See?"

"Wow," Abel said dryly.

"I called Griff too."

"Oh, Justin." Grey stopped and hugged him.

"He lives in Portland, but we're going to meet up in a few weeks. I just need some time to process things."

"That makes sense." Abel nodded, then tugged Justin again. "Let's get inside."

"Why are you all here anyway?" Tanner grinned when they glared at him. "Not that we aren't happy to see you."

"You two got away with a private wedding, but you can't avoid the reception," Caden answered as he approached. "The pub closed for the afternoon so that we could welcome you all home."

"Food? I'm in." Justin headed toward the pub with his friends. He looked over his shoulder and gave Tanner a heated look.

Tanner followed.

A buffet of delicious food greeted them, along with their friends and family. A banner hung across the bar, and balloons filled the air above them. Music played and people already danced in the middle of the room.

"They're here!" Abel jumped up and grabbed a balloon. He handed it to them. "Congratulations, guys."

Justin took it and laughed. "Thanks. Where's the food?"

"Reuben was in earlier, but he already left. The man

really doesn't like crowds." Abel waved to the table. "For the main dish, we have slow-cooked tri-tips and beef short ribs. Then there are mashed potatoes, beer-battered asparagus, and a million other side dishes. Reuben even made brussel sprouts, and I have to admit they're good."

"Abuela and I made your cake." Grey handed Justin Auggie and showed them the large, three-tier cake.

"You guys are the best." Tanner wrapped an arm around his omega's waist and looked around the room.

Travis and a few other guys had filled in for him at the last minute, and the Wilsons had chipped in with the pub. Now, this.

The next few hours flew by. They ate delicious food and caught up with everyone, and Tanner enjoyed dancing with his omega, even if Auggie was between them the whole time.

"Gift time!" Grey pulled them from the dance floor and brought them to the bar.

The bar was covered with presents, and Justin wiped his eyes. "You all didn't need to get us anything."

Abel scoffed. "It's like you don't know us at all. Here. Open mine first."

They sat and started opening presents. Tanner arched a brow and held up a pair of silky blue manties. "Really, Abel?"

"Those are for Justin." Abel hesitated. "Well, if you want to try them, you can, but are you the same size?"

Justin snickered and grabbed the manties. "He's a boxer briefs kind of guy."

Grey laughed and showed him a picture. "This is from Harper and I."

"Another bunny?" Tanner looked over Justin's shoulder.

The picture was of a king-sized, handcrafted bed frame. "Oh, thank god."

"Hey now," Grey said. "Butter Bunny would like a little brother or sister."

"Well, that brings up my gift." Dr. Grover and his ladies stepped forward and handed him a black and white guinea pig in a unicorn costume.

"Uh..." Tanner tilted his head.

Justin started laughing. "You found me a unicorn."

"We have toys here too, and Carter put together a huge guinea pig home." Grover smiled hopefully. "Butter Bunny loves him too. They've had daily playdates."

Tanner held the guinea pig up and looked it over. "That'll do, pig. That'll do."

Grammy chuckled. "I don't know if we can top that present, but we got you guys something too."

Gramps held up a large, handmade cubby shelf. "You can put Justin's snow globes in it."

Grammy handed Justin a wrapped gift. "You could put this in it too."

Justin gave her a questioning look and unwrapped the gift and gasped. It was a photo of his mom in a handmade frame. Rhonda was smiling wide and laughing. Her blond hair blew around her face, and her green eyes danced.

"It's beautiful," Justin said, covering his mouth. "Definitely going in the shelf. Thank you, Grammy."

She hugged him. "We love you, sweetie. You and Tanner have a beautiful life ahead of you."

"Thank you too, Gramps." Tanner sniffed and gave the older man a half hug. "We appreciate you two."

"Fucking Wilsons and your sweetness." Justin wiped his eyes and looked around the room. "I hate you all."

"We can tell," North said dryly. "This is from all of us at

The Irish Rose." He handed a wrapped present to Justin, since Tanner's hands were full of a guinea pig unicorn.

Justin clapped excitedly and opened the gift. "Oh, my god. I've wanted this set of dishes forever."

"We noticed," Laura said, laughing.

"You talked about them all the time," Albie added with a grin. "Then you would sigh and say they were just too expensive."

"Thanks, guys." Justin's eyes watered again. "You all are so great."

They finished opening presents eventually, then served the cake. Tanner and Justin snuggled together in one chair, and Justin gave him a soft kiss.

"I love you, Tanner Jones."

"I love you too, Justin Jones."

"Even if your parents don't approve of us?"

"Fuck them. I know you, Justin. I see the man you are, and I love you more than anything. I am so happy."

"Hey guys." Sheriff McKenzie sat next to them. "I have a spot of good news."

"Does it involve Wally and Chelsea?" Tanner smirked.

"How did you guess?" McKenzie arched a brow. "Chelsea will do time, but she gave us what we needed to catch Wally. She had a bunch of pills stashed here that she was selling to your less-than-savory customers. Wally was supplying her. He was also the one to sell your mom those pills, and he'll get jailtime for distributing."

"Tanner? You knew about this?" Justin looked at him with wide eyes.

"Yeah. I wasn't sure what would happen, so I didn't want to get your hopes up."

Justin kissed him. "Thank you, handsome. It helps knowing Wally is being held accountable. I know Mom was responsible for herself, but Wally is a manipulative asshole."

"Do I get a kiss?" McKenzie fluttered his eyes.

"Sure thing." Tanner leaned over and gave him a big smooch on his cheek.

"Ugh." McKenzie scrubbed his cheek, and they laughed at him.

"See how much I love you, honey?" Tanner kissed his omega again.

Their new guinea pig rolled by in a guinea pig ball. Rue and some other children ran after him.

"Even if Doc gave us a guinea pig dressed as a unicorn?"

Tanner laughed. "Even then, maybe especially then."

"Butter Bunny needs to be here. It's only fair. I'll be right back." Abel ran toward the kitchen.

"What are you going to name him?" Caden waved toward the guinea pig.

Tanner considered their new pet when he rolled by again. "Hmm. How about Buttons? Then we'd have Buttons and Butter Bunny."

Justin pulled him down for another kiss. "I like that."

Before Tanner could insist on more kisses, he noticed an unfamiliar man at the front door. The large alpha had spiky dark hair and warm brown skin. He was covered in tattoos and piercings.

"Hey, the pub is closed until four." Caden gave the man a friendly smile.

"Oh. Sorry, man. I'm the new bartender and wanted to scope the place out." The man winced, then turned to leave.

"Wait." Justin waved his arms. "Come on in. I'm Justin, one of the owners, and I have to say we are so happy to have you."

"Reuben said you all were hurting for help." He smiled

at Justin and ambled over. "I really am sorry to interrupt. What's the party for?"

"Tanner and I ran off to Vegas to get married." Justin stuck his hand out and wiggled his fingers. "Isn't my ring beautiful?"

"Sparkly." The man grinned. "Congrats."

"That's an awful lot of piercings you have there." Grammy looked the man over. "Wild man, hmm?"

"Grammy!" Janelle, one of her granddaughters, sounded annoyed. "Don't make assumptions."

Grammy looked at her fondly. "You're right, baby girl."

The man winced. "Well, to be honest, I was pretty wild until a few years ago."

"I was right! It's that look in your eye." Grammy smiled, pleased. "You're going to give someone trouble. I just know it."

Justin rolled his eyes and waved the man to a seat as the party resumed.

"Come on, sunshine." Harper handed Auggie to Ernie and pulled Grey to the dance floor.

"Why did you want to leave the Caribbean?" Ernie watched the stranger curiously as he cuddled Auggie close.

The man's smile held a secret. Tanner wondered what was behind it. "Several reasons, really."

"How mysterious." Grammy looked at him suspiciously. "Are you running from a wife? Maybe two that didn't know about each other. They found out and you needed to start over somewhere else to avoid caring for your ten children."

The man laughed loudly while everyone else gave Grammy sour looks.

"Fine, fine. I won't assume things." She threw her hands up.

The man's laughter turned to chuckles. "My main reason involves a delicious omega."

"I told you he was going to be someone's trouble." Grammy looked smug.

"Another reason is my parents died."

"Oh, sweetie." Grammy moved from her seat and hugged him. "I'm sorry."

Justin shot the man a sympathetic look. Tanner kissed his neck. It was easy to push Rhonda's death to the back of their minds with everything else happening, but in quiet moments, it still knocked the breath out of them. Tanner knew it would for a long time.

"Thanks. We weren't exactly close, but I have a little sister. I have custody of her now as well as my son. When Reuben told me about this place, I knew it was the place for us." The man smiled his secret smile again.

"How do you know Reuben? I love the man, but he isn't too talkative." Justin finished off his cake, then grabbed Tanner's and started in on it.

"He's a quiet one," the man agreed. "We were in the Navy together and kept in touch after leaving."

"I didn't know he was in the Navy." Justin sounded disgruntled. He put the empty plate down on the table.

"Most of us haven't even met the man yet." Ernie handed Justin Auggie again. "He runs as soon as we arrive."

"He's a good guy, but he does like his space." The man shrugged.

Tanner cleared his throat. "I'm Tanner, by the way. I'm sorry, but I don't know your name."

"Oh, yeah. I guess Reuben wouldn't have said." The man shook his head. "I'm—"

"Mateo?" Abel's voice was loud and surprised.

Mateo's eyes filled with heat, and he jumped up, starting toward him. "Thought you'd get away, mi alma?"

Abel stood in shock, holding Butter Bunny to his chest. "How did you know where I was?"

Mateo didn't answer him. He pulled Abel into his arms and kissed him deeply.

Abel didn't seem to mind. He wrapped an arm around Mateo's neck and moaned as he kissed him back.

"Oh, dear." Grammy smiled wide. "I told you that man would be trouble. Handsome and devilish trouble."

Tanner shared a look with his omega. "The best kind."

PART IV

Grey's Gift
A Hobson Hills Short
Hobson Hills Omegas: Book 6.5

AUTHOR'S NOTE

"Grey's Gift" is book 6.5 in the Hobson Hills Omegas series.
The events in this short story occur after those in *Unraveling
the Omega*.

20

ELIJAH AND CARTER

Elijah stood on the porch of his old farmhouse and danced in place. "Come on, baby boys. Shake those butts."

His twin boys twisted their hips and pumped their arms in the air. Cooper, Elijah's omega son, had his daddy's style. His little nose was scrunched up, and he put everything he had into shaking his butt. The long earflaps of his knitted hat swung back and forth. "Look it, Daddy!"

Connor giggled, watching his brother. Elijah's alpha son was a little more reserved and slowly swayed back and forth, clutching Hotdog's side to keep balance. Carter's Old English sheepdog stood patiently next to the little boy.

Their smaller miniature schnauzer was the smart one. Winston was inside, curled up on a soft dog bed next to the fireplace.

"You boys are perfect," Elijah said. "Are you ready to go feed the beasts?"

"Come on, Boo," Cooper said and waved at the black cat perched on the porch rail. "Moo moo, baa baa."

"Squawk," Connor yelled loudly, laughing.

Elijah shook his head and laughed. "You silly boys."

He helped them down the steps, and they danced together toward the barn. Elijah couldn't stop grinning. By late November, all hints of autumn in Maine were long gone. It was cold and wet outside with a thick layer of snow on the ground, but he had his boys with him, and Carter and Olive would be home in a few hours.

They reached the barn, and Banjo brayed loudly, head hanging over his stall. Pooka followed suit and gave them a soft moo.

"Pooka," Connor said loudly, dancing to his favorite animal. "Moo, Pooka." The Jersey cow nosed his head and mooed.

Coop danced wildly to Billy's stall and paused to scratch the goat's forehead. "Billy."

The goat bleated gently.

Wayne and Garth watched them from their joint stall. The Scottish Highland heifer's hair fell into her eyes. She leaned down so Connor could pet her nose. "Pretty Wayne."

The grey llama clucked and waited his turn. Elijah picked his son up, so he could pet the llama's head.

"You good boy, Garth," Connor said.

Cooper giggled as he ran past them, chasing their only chicken – a small, Polish hen. Tinka had the run of the barn and enjoyed laying her egg in different spots each day. Coop enjoyed trying to find it.

"Snuggles turn," Connor said, patting Elijah's cheek.

He carried his son over to the last stall. Their single sheep baaed impatiently from her stall. She loved Connor time. Elijah sat with Connor, and the two of them pampered the little sheep for a few minutes.

"You play with Hotdog while I feed the beasts, alright?"

"'Kay."

Coop was still giggling as he ran past them again, this time being chased by Tinka.

Elijah smiled happily and took care of the animals. He refilled their hay and checked on the water. He noted the state of their stalls. Carter and Olive would be mucking stalls tonight. Usually, the animals stayed out in the huge field behind the barn, but none of their spoiled brats liked the snow. They preferred the comfort of their stalls.

Elijah quickly milked Pooka and Wayne, then set it in the freezer. His sons were dancing with Hotdog and Boo in the barn's walkway, and Coop waved a small, white egg at him.

"Come on, boys. Back to the house to wash those hands. Coop, *do not* put that egg in your mouth."

Coop sighed but held the egg carefully in his mitten-covered hands. "Tinka says I can."

"Tinka isn't your daddy, is she?"

"No." Coop pouted. They danced back to the house and up the back steps to the kitchen.

Coop handed Elijah the egg and hugged Hotdog. "Hotdog play!"

"Take your coats off first and wash your hands," Elijah ordered.

"Potty, Daddy," Connor said as soon as his coat and gloves were off.

Elijah helped his son to the bathroom and clapped when Connor climbed the little steps and sat on the toilet all by himself. "You're such a good boy!"

"I potty too," Coop said grumpily.

Elijah winced and picked him up, running upstairs to the hall bathroom. Many an accident had occurred when both boys had to potty at the same time. "Hold it, baby boy."

Emergency averted, Elijah helped them wash their

hands and settle down to play on the living room floor. He pulled his laptop out and checked his e-mail. After answering several student e-mails, he checked his personal account, and one message in particular caught his eyes. His friend Melinda worked with a small publishing firm in Boston.

Elijah,

Your cousin is driving me crazy! My boss wants to publish Grey's books, but he keeps putting me off. They're so good, Eli. We've offered him more money, looser commitments, basically anything he wants. Talk some sense into him!

Mel

"Hmm." Elijah grabbed his phone and called Harper.

"Hey, Elijah." Harper sounded happy. "How's it going?"

"Why won't Grey publish his children's books? Olive and the boys love them. Your kids love them. Yeo and Dean's kids love them. Everyone loves them!"

Harper groaned. "I think he's afraid. He puts so much of himself into them, and that first publisher he talked to was so critical. It kind of put him off even trying. You know how hard it was to get him to let your friend Melinda look at them."

Elijah tapped his chin. "I regret recommending Dave. I knew him from college, but he's turned into a big poopy head."

"A big poopy head?" Harper sounded amused.

"You have kids. You know what I really want to call him."

Harper snorted. "Good point."

Elijah watched the boys play for a moment. "I have an idea. I think it's time for a Wilson family intervention."

"Huh?"

"Just trust me and check your e-mail tonight." Elijah ended the call and started planning. The world needed

Grey's books, and Elijah was going to make sure his friend knew it.

———

CARTER SCRATCHED his head and watched his husband stuff Winston into the frog costume. He loved Elijah and knew his omega was the smartest person in the world, but Carter was confused. "Explain why we're dressing the kids and our pets up as characters in Grey's books again?"

"Dad," Olive said, hands on her hips. She was dressed as a witch in a long purple robe. "We told you already. Cousin Grey needs to know we love his books and they're good, so we're going to act out scenes, so he'll see it."

Connor switched his plastic sword around. "I'm prince!"

Olive smiled fondly at the little guy. "You're the hero, Connor. Boo and I are going to help you and Hotdog save Winston from the frog curse."

Carter laughed. Hotdog wore a horse costume and followed Connor around, ever the faithful steed. Poor Boo wore a little witch's hat. She would play the part of the witch's pet familiar.

"Rawr!" Coop ran into the room, carrying Hodges with him. Carter wasn't sure why Coop was roaring. Their youngest was dressed as an adorable, er, fierce dark wizard. Hodges and Ham and Eggs the Fourth would be his minions.

Ham rolled into the room in his hamster ball, and Carter lost it, laughing hard. "Is he supposed to be a zombie?"

Coop held Hodges up. The hedgehog wore a wizard's hat. "Hodges my friend. We lead undead."

Elijah started giggling. "Okay. It really is adorable."

Coop stomped his foot. "Scary!"

Carter snorted as he laughed harder. "So scary."

He pulled Elijah into his arms, and they watched the kids. Olive moved everyone to their places, patiently explaining to Connor that he couldn't hold his brother's hand.

"No. I love Coopy. We hold hands." Connor's face turned stubborn.

Olive threw her hands up. "Fine, but that's not how the story goes."

"New story," Coop said, wiggling. "Love Conni."

Carter nuzzled his husband's neck. "Our kids are the best kids in the world."

"You may be a little biased."

Carter shook his head. He knew he was a lucky man. His Olive was a smart and kind little girl. The boys looked just like their daddy and had hearts as big as the moon.

Elijah leaned up and kissed his chin. "Okay, kids. Let's take our pictures for Cousin Grey. He needs to know how great his story is."

"I liked this one the best," Olive said, helping Carter move Hotdog into place. "He wrote it for me."

"He sure did," Carter said and tugged her long dark braid.

They took pictures, then changed the poses and took even more. Ham and Eggs kept running away, so Hotdog had to do a little herding. After an hour, everyone was tired and grumpy, but they had a lot of cute pictures for Grey's gift.

Carter noted how wiped Elijah looked and clapped his hands. "Alright. Olive, you and I are putting the boys to bed, then helping the pets out of their costumes."

"Potty," Connor said, tugging on his leg.

Carter grinned. "You got it, buddy. Let's go potty."

Coop stomped his foot. "Me potty too."

Olive snickered. "Come on, Coop. I'll help you."

After he got the kids into bed, then rescued the pets from their costumes, he hugged Olive goodnight and made his way to the master bedroom.

His omega was still warm and flushed from the shower. Elijah was curled up on the bed, scrolling through pictures on his phone. "I'll get some good shots of our barn pets tomorrow. They can be part of Coop's undead army."

Carter crawled across him and gave him a hot, wet kiss. "How you feeling, baby?"

Elijah's eyes closed, and he smiled, snuggling into Carter's lap, then pressed his ear against Carter's chest.

"You listening to my heartbeat again?"

"It's always there, nice and steady."

Carter cupped Elijah's face and stroked a thumb under his eye. "You seem tired, Elijah. Was today busy?"

"Not more than usual." Elijah watched him, eyes serious. "Olive is doing well in school and has plenty of friends. The twins are almost completely potty-trained."

"Okay?"

"I'm pregnant, Carter."

Carter choked on his spit and coughed harshly, so Elijah leaned up and patted his back. "Pregnant? We're having another baby?"

Elijah grinned, a teasing light in his eyes. "Did the idea make you choke up? You must really like it."

Carter laughed, voice cracking. His omega and his family were everything to him. "We're having another baby, Elijah." His brain seemed stuck on those words. They filled his mind, repeating over and over again. *We're having another baby.*

"How do you feel about it?" Elijah's freckled nose called

to him, so Carter leaned down and kissed it. "Don't try to distract me, love muffin. Answer the question."

Carter smirked and arched an eyebrow. "Love muffin?"

Elijah sniffed. "I like it. Now, do you want another baby?"

Carter closed his eyes and thought about it. Their days were full with work and the kids they had now, but it was nice to hold Grey and Harper's youngest, Auggie. He had that new baby smell and the sweetest disposition. It would also make his omega happy and that was Carter's main goal in life. Tomás was fully trained and was a big help with C&J Plumbing and Contracting, so Carter could have a little more free time.

He opened his eyes. "I'm good with another baby. I can be home more to help this time."

Elijah grinned, happy. "Perfect."

GREY AND HARPER

Grey leaned back in his office chair and stretched his arms over his head. Another website design was submitted. His client hadn't given him much to work with, but at least, he didn't seem too picky.

He looked around. The room was too quiet. Harper had taken Rue, Auggie, and all the pets to the workshop today so Grey could work, but Grey missed the noise. He quickly checked through his e-mail, stomach growling. He was ready for lunch.

"Not again." Melinda Turbell was persistent and kept his mailbox full.

He rubbed his face and leaned back in his chair. He remembered when he talked to the first publisher almost three years ago. They had acted interested in his books, but when he met face to face with Dave Jones, everything had changed. *Stick to websites, Mr. Wilson.*

Grey shook his head, trying to shake the words out of his mind. He liked his books, damn it. He enjoyed making them, and his sons seemed to like them too. It didn't matter that they weren't good enough to publish. Hell, he didn't have the time to deal with that anyway.

"It's too quiet." Grey moaned when his stomach growled again. He left the office and went downstairs, only tripping over three toys along the way. Rue still hadn't quite grasped the concept of cleaning up after himself.

He made a sandwich and warmed up a bowl of the homemade chicken noodle soup from yesterday. As soon as he sat at the table, he noticed the cars parked near Harper's workshop.

"Why are Shawn and Abuela here?" Grey asked aloud. Abuela would normally come straight to the house when she visited. He supposed she knew Harper had the kids. His eyes narrowed when he noticed Ernie leaving the workshop with a large bag. Harper's cousin looked around furtively and hurriedly stuffed the bag in the trunk of Shawn's car. "What's going on?"

Grey finished his lunch and washed the dishes before walking to the workshop, boots sinking into the crisp snow. He was about halfway there when Rue pushed open the barn door and ran outside.

"Daddy, no! Stay in the house."

His eldest son was a dark-skinned, dark-haired cutie, all bundled up for winter. "What's going on, Rue?"

Rue's eyes widened. "It's secret! You can't go in there."

"Is it a Christmas present?"

Rue scrunched up his nose. "Not really. Hug me!"

Grey laughed. "You and your dad know just how to distract me."

Rue wiggled his arms. "Hugs!"

Grey leaned down and hugged his big boy. "You're getting so tall, Rue. Soon, you'll be as tall as the barn."

It was so strange to think he'd been pregnant with this

stinker and worrying himself to death three years ago. He'd been so alone and scared before Harper brought him home. Now he had a wonderful husband, a precocious preschooler, and a sweet baby.

"Sunshine, what are you doing out here?" Harper smiled nervously. His alpha wasn't good at subterfuge, and Grey could read him like a book.

Grey arched an eyebrow. "What's going on here?"

Harper strode from the barn and pulled Grey and Rue into his arms. "You look beautiful today, Sunshine."

Grey snorted. "You think I look beautiful every day. What are you up to?"

Harper gave him an innocent look. "Me? Nothing at all. Why don't we let Shawn take Rue here, and you and I will go get some lunch in town."

Shawn was suddenly there. "Hey, Grey. Come on, Rue. Let's go play with the bunnies."

Grey crossed his arms. "I already ate lunch."

Harper swallowed hard and looked around nervously. "What about a doughnut from Honey Buns?"

Grey laughed. "You know my love for doughnuts knows no bounds."

Harper took his hand and tugged him toward the truck. "Shawn, you know what to do."

The younger man laughed and picked Rue up, slinging him over his shoulder. "Sure thing. Come on, bud. Let's take care of business."

Rue watched Grey while Shawn carried him back to the barn. "Bring me back a doughnut, Daddy!"

"He's my son, alright." Grey caught Harper's face in his hands and kissed him. "I love you, Harper, even though you're hiding something."

Harper just grinned and helped him into the truck. They

drove toward town, and Grey admired the snowy scenery around them. He was finally starting to adjust to the cold winters, but he still hated driving on icy roads.

"Did you read Rue's preschool report card?" Grey asked. "I left it on the table last night."

Harper grinned at him. "I did. I'm sorry I had to work late last night."

"You had a lot of orders to fill." Grey took Harper's hand in his and studied his alpha's nimble fingers. "What did you think of Ms. Annie's comments?"

"I know it's just preschool, but I'm so proud of Rue. Do you think we ought to move him to their full day program? She said he's doing really well, but it will be five days and a full six hours each day."

"I don't know. Yeo is only now moving Linc to the full day program, and he'll start kindergarten next year." Grey sighed. "Damn it. I miss our little booger when he's gone, but Elijah told me Ms. Darcy does a special Spanish or French lesson every Tuesday and Thursday with her group. She even has a cultural day on Fridays."

Harper groaned. "Rue would love that."

"He loves languages." Grey smiled. Abuela enjoyed teaching Rue new Spanish words and always told him stories about the small Argentinian town she'd been born in. His son soaked it all up like a sponge.

"If you agree, then let's do it," Harper said. "I don't want to hold our boy back just because we'll miss him. I can't believe he's turning three in two weeks."

"At least, we have a couple more years with Auggie." Grey's younger son was just a little over six months.

"So, I heard that Melinda Turbell sent you another offer," Harper said suddenly.

Grey frowned. How had Harper heard that? Grey hadn't told anyone else about the offers. "How?"

Harper winced and tapped his fingers on the steering wheel. "Elijah may have mentioned it. Melinda is a friend of his."

"Is that why she keeps e-mailing me? Is she doing Elijah a favor?"

Harper rolled his eyes. "No. Elijah was raving about one of your books, and she asked about it. Then she wanted to know about the others. She really seems genuine."

Grey shrugged. "Elijah was friends with the last one too."

Harper growled. "Not anymore."

"Anyway, it doesn't matter. I'm happy writing for just the family."

Harper squeezed his hand. "Hmm, okay. So, what kind of doughnut are you getting?"

Grey gave his husband a confused look. "All the doughnuts. You know me, Harper. Why would you ask me to choose?"

<hr>

HARPER WATCHED Grey devour a plate of doughnuts. It really couldn't be healthy for one person to eat that many doughnuts all at once, but he wasn't stupid enough to say that aloud.

Grey took a sip of his coffee. "So, you're really not going to tell me what you're up to in the barn?"

Harper grinned. His omega looked adorably grumpy. "Not at all."

His favorite book by Grey was called *Rue and Mr. Bear*. It was a cute story about a little boy that meets an injured bear in the woods. After the boy helps the bear, they become best friends.

With Shawn and Ernie's help, Harper had dressed Rue, Auggie, and all their pets as characters from the book. Then they had taken a bunch of pictures.

Even Ines, Grey's abuela, had gotten involved and dressed like a park ranger. Rue had played the role of Rue, of course, and Auggie had gotten to play a friendly owl.

Grey's large Newfoundland, Chewie, hadn't exactly enjoyed his role as the bear, and Tiny, their Maine Coon cat, had been forced into a wolf costume. Harper felt a little guilty for forcing the feline to play along.

Opal, their smaller dog, and Butterball, their miniature pig, had been dressed as squirrels. Those two were so used to wearing pet costumes that they hadn't blinked an eye. Harper's two Shetland ponies, on the other hand, hadn't wanted to wear deer costumes. They were work horses, not actors. The rabbits had the easiest role. They each had played the role of rabbit very well, no costumes needed.

It had taken a lot of effort, but they had gotten several good pictures. Harper trusted Shawn to finish the job while he distracted Grey.

"Grey, why won't you let Melinda at least publish one of your books?" Harper couldn't help but ask. "It would just be one, and you could see how it went before you put the rest out there."

Grey groaned. "You'll think I'm stupid."

Harper scooted out of his seat and sat beside Grey, wrapping an arm around him. "That will never happen, sunshine."

"You're so... you," Grey said, waving his hand in the air. "You're confident and comfortable in your own skin. I don't know if you'll understand it."

Harper shrugged. "You know that wasn't always the case."

"Yeah, you're right." Grey propped his chin on his fist and started on another doughnut. "I've always played it safe, even before my family died. I never took many chances."

Harper smirked. "You took one on me, and we're happy."

Grey laughed. "Yes, we are." He looked thoughtful for a moment. "When I graduated college, I was so lucky to get the job I did. I like web design. It lets me be creative to a degree, and I make good money."

Harper sat up straight. "Like isn't love."

Grey set his head on Harper's shoulder, and Harper couldn't resist kissing the top of his omega's head.

"I *love* making children's books," Grey whispered. "Right now, I can make them and no one judges if they're good or bad. There's no risk. I can always say it's just a hobby."

"Sometimes, it's worth it to take a chance," Harper said. "When I started selling my furniture, I was afraid no one would buy it. I put my soul into building things, and, to most people, it's just a chair or a table."

"Your work is art," Grey said, growling. "Anyone who doesn't appreciate that is an idiot."

Harper hid his grin. He loved it when his cute omega got growly. "It was hard at first to put it out there. Then Dr. Grover came by and ordered a custom-sized bedframe."

Grey snickered. "For him and his two ladies."

Harper laughed. "Yeah. I prefer to think he's using that bed for innocent snuggling."

Grey laughed so hard he almost choked on a piece of doughnut. Harper patted his back and waited until the man was composed.

"When he saw what I created, Doc was really impressed. That made me feel so damn good, Grey. Of course, not everyone loves my work and not everyone will love your books. Someone will though. Our family does, that's for sure, but there's a kid out there that will read about Rue and Mr. Bear and fall in love. Their imagination will let them go along on Rue's adventures, and there's no telling where it will take them. That's what your books will do. All you have to do is take a chance."

Grey buried his face against Harper's shoulder. "I love you, Harper Wilson."

"I love you too, sunshine."

Grey's head shot up, and he glared at the man a few tables down from them. "Isn't that Luke Jennings?"

Harper looked over his shoulder. "Looks like it. Oh, damn. Is he on a date? I thought he was seeing Justin's brother Griff." The couple leaned in close and kissed. Yeah, Luke and the woman were definitely on a date.

"That asshole," Grey hissed. "Let's kick his butt."

Harper patted Grey's back. "Hold on, sunshine. Luke isn't the type to cheat on someone. Let's go ask Jackson. Griff and he are good friends."

Grey huffed, then stuffed the last doughnut in his mouth while Harper cleaned their table. Jackson worked at The Book Worm, right next door.

The young omega was ringing up a customer at the register when they approached. Jackson looked a bit like his papa, but his dark green eyes and freckles came from his father. Luckily, Harper knew that was all Jackson got from his alphahole father.

Jackson looked up, grinning. "Hey, you two."

Grey leaned against the counter once the customer left. "Jackson, is Griff dating Luke Jennings?"

Jackson scrunched his nose. "Uh, no."

Harper breathed a sigh of relief. He really didn't want to

have to kick someone's ass today. He knew that if he didn't defend Griff's honor, Grey would.

Grey tilted his head, eyes confused. "Really? Abel said he saw those two kissing at the pub."

Jackson blushed. "Geez, talk about small town life, right?"

Harper snorted. "Privacy is just a myth, Jackson. You've lived here long enough to know that."

Jackson grinned and leaned toward Grey. "Luke and Griff really are just friends. We all hang out. Griff and he fooled around a little, but Luke met a girl named Britney and is crazy about her."

Grey pursed his lips. "Oh. Well, he's on a date with someone now."

Jackson's eyes lit up. "Really?" He rushed to the doorway to Honey Buns and looked inside. "That's her! That's Britney. Aww, don't they look cute together? I'm taking pictures and sending them to Griff. We've been trying to get Luke to make a move for weeks."

Grey looked a little sad. "So no broken-hearted Griff? What about you?"

Jackson rolled his eyes and went back to the register. "No, dork. I'm never trusting anyone with my heart. There are too many assholes out there."

Harper bit his lip. He could have sworn he'd seen something in Jackson's eyes when he'd spoken with a certain alpha at Grammy's Sunday breakfasts.

Grey tugged on his arm. "Has enough time passed for us to go home?"

Harper checked his watch. "Yep. Let's go, sunshine. I need to hug Auggie."

22

DAVID AND SAWYER

"Penelope, don't chew on Chunky's tail," David said, snapping a quick picture of his youngest daughter. She wore rabbit ears and a cute knitted rabbit costume. All of the animals and kids were dressed like rabbits. David's favorite book by Grey was about a family of rabbits that moved from the country to the city.

"Daddy, hungry." Phinn looked like a sad rabbit. His lip trembled, and one rabbit ear drooped down to cover his eyes.

"Seriously, Dad. It's been hours. I don't think Elijah meant for us to perfectly enact the whole book in a photoshoot." David's eldest kid, Sadie, tugged at her rabbit sweater. "You promised us pizza."

"Pizza," Penelope and Phinn yelled together.

Sawyer, David's husband, glared at Sadie. "You know better than to say that word."

Sadie smirked, then shrugged. "Oops."

"Dad," Ryder said. "Who makes the better rabbit, Chunky or Cadbury?"

Sawyer laughed. "I think Cadbury wins this one, since he's actually a rabbit."

Harry covered the rabbit's long ears. "Dad, don't say that. Cadbury is a cat like Chunky, remember? Be respectful."

Sawyer gave their son a serious look, eyes twinkling. "You're right. I'm so sorry."

David hid his smile. "Babe, fix Mo's ears." The Border Collie's rabbit ears were slipping off his head. The dog gave him an unamused look. "I'm sorry, Mo. One more shoot and we'll go get dinner."

"Pwomise?" Phinn had the most pitiful puppy dog eyes in the world.

"I promise." David fixed his camera and quickly ran through the last scene in the book.

As soon as he set his phone down, his kids made a break for it, pulling off rabbit ears and tossing them aside.

"I'll order the pizza," Sawyer said, kissing David's cheek.

David watched his man go, admiring Sawyer's nice firm ass.

Sadie elbowed him in the side. "You two are disgusting."

David made a face and slipped his heels off before pulling Sadie to the couch. "Are you forgetting I caught you and Garrett the Hottie making out in the driveway Saturday night?"

Sadie leaned down and picked up Daisy. "Okay, okay. You didn't tell Dad, did you?"

David smoothed a hand over his short hair. "Of course I did. Then I talked him out of going to the poor boy's house and murdering him. You should bring Garrett over for dinner."

Sadie groaned. "It's not like that. We like each other, but it's senior year. It would be stupid to start something right now. He's going to a school in Colorado, and I'm doing University of Maine."

David leaned his arm on the back of the couch. "That's no reason not to date."

Sadie made a face. "Marsha Dixon said as soon as she turns eighteen, she and Todd are getting married. She's had a boyfriend constantly since she turned thirteen. I don't want to be like that. I'm good on my own. If I meet someone at school next year, then okay, just not right now."

David sighed. "Okay. I won't push you since you're being all sensible and shit. You need to tell Marsha that eighteen is too young to get married."

Sadie shrugged. "It's seems natural for her. All her life, she's dreamed of being someone's girlfriend or wife."

"Hmm," David said, trying not to judge. He reminded himself that every person was different. "How are your duel enrollment classes going?"

"Statistics is just fine, but English is boring. It's just about writing papers."

"Count yourself lucky and hope it doesn't get more difficult." David reached out and tugged a strand of her long hair. "Thank you for doing the photoshoot."

Sadie grinned. "Grey will love it. I hope this gift works. His books are so good, and the world needs to see them."

"I agree," Sawyer said, dropping into the seat beside David. "Pizza will be here soon."

Ryder groaned and sat in one of the chairs near the window, Phinn in his lap. "Chunky likes his costume. He won't take it off."

"This is why I'm only taking Mo with me when I move out next year," Sadie said, sniffing. "My dog is smart enough to know costumes are stupid."

Ryder laughed. "You're taking Mo because you can't live

without him. Plus, Daisy is my cat, Chunky is Harry's, and Cadbury is Dad's."

Sawyer groaned and hid his face against David's shoulder. "Can we please not talk about Sadie moving out?"

David chuckled. Sadie had decided to get an apartment close to the university with a few of her friends. Thankfully, her college fund would allow her to live off-campus and commute.

Sadie smacked her dad's knee. "Give me a few years and I'll be graduating and becoming a nurse. Then what will you do, Dad?"

Sawyer smiled softly. "Be proud as hell. We have good kids."

"That we do," David agreed.

Harry chased a giggling Penelope into the living room. "Pizza, pizza, pizza, pizza."

David smiled. Maybe he should have fed them before the photoshoot.

SAWYER CLOSED the door to the twins' bedroom as quietly as he could. His sock-covered feet were almost silent as he made his way down the hall, checking on each of the kids along the way.

Ryder was propped up, reading a book with Daisy curled beside him. Harry was already asleep, snoring softly against Chunky's fur. Sadie was typing something into her phone, earbuds nestled in her ears. Mo slept on his back at the foot of her bed.

Sawyer didn't want to think about Sadie going away next year. She was so beautiful and sweet. He didn't want the world to have a chance at hurting her.

He opened the door to his and David's room. His beta husband was sprawled on his stomach, feet in the air. Light glinted off his bright red toe nails.

David looked over his shoulder. "Are we going to talk about Jill?"

Sawyer sighed and flopped onto the bed next to him. "Do you really think she'll come?"

David nodded. "I do. She doesn't make empty promises, and she really wants us all to meet the new husband."

Sawyer rubbed his face. Jill called weekly to talk to the kids and stayed updated on their lives. She also contributed to all of their college funds and paid child support. Despite all of that, she struggled to really connect with the kids.

Ryder and Harry didn't seem to mind. They liked talking to her, but they had no trouble hanging up the phone. Sadie, on the other hand, still barely spoke to her mother.

"What about Sadie's graduation?" Sawyer would much rather Jill come for that than for Christmas.

"She says she wants to do both." David propped his head on his fist. "I don't think she's going to come for Christmas every year or anything, but she really does want the kids to meet Jean Luc. I do, however, think she'll come to each of their high school graduations. Probably college graduations too."

"I just don't want her to say she'll come, then not come."

"I know what you mean," David said, rolling on top of him. "I don't want the kids to get their feelings hurt either."

"She *is* careful about what she says," Sawyer said slowly, running his hands over David's generous ass.

David kissed him, tongue pushing past his lips. Sawyer's dick went from soft to hard in thirty seconds. David spread his legs and straddled Sawyer's lap, pressing their erections together.

"I love you," David whispered against his mouth. "Forget everything else and fuck me into the mattress."

Sawyer moaned and rolled David beneath him, pressing kisses along his husband's neck and chest. "Fuck, I love your taste."

Sawyer took his time, nibbling every inch of David's delicious skin. He made his way slowly down his body, licking, kissing, and biting until his man was writhing beneath him.

Finally, Sawyer pumped David's dick and licked the tip. David grabbed his head and lifted his hips, making Sawyer smile. He swallowed the tip of his husband's dick and slowly slid his mouth down as far as it could go.

After a few minutes of stretching and lube, Sawyer slid inside David, relishing the tight heat of his ass. He went slow, hands gripping David's hips as he pushed in, then slid out, over and over again.

David pulled him down for a kiss, mouth panting against his. "You feel so fucking good inside me."

Sawyer started moving faster, pressing his forehead to David's. The moved together perfectly, bodies fitting just right against each other's. David came all over Sawyer's hand, and Sawyer couldn't hold out any longer. He shuddered and came.

They watched one another as they caught their breath. This was the part Sawyer liked best. The way David watched him made him feel as if he could fly.

The next morning, Sawyer dropped the kids off at school and stopped by Honey Buns for coffee. Zoe Wilson owned the place and was a queen as far as Sawyer was concerned.

"Hey, handsome," the lovely woman said. "You want your usual?"

He smiled. "Please."

As Zoe worked on his coffee, he noticed her shoulders were stiff and her face looked strained. "What's wrong, Zo?"

She put the two drinks in a small carrier and bagged up a few pieces of biscotti before answering him. "It's Gib's mother. She won't take his calls and avoids him anytime we see her in public. He tried going to her house yesterday, and she wouldn't let him in."

Sawyer squeezed her hand. "If she doesn't accept Gib as he is, then it's her loss. We'll be here for you and him both."

She smiled sadly. "Thanks. It wouldn't bother me, except it hurts him so much." She shook herself and took a breath. "Okay. Enough of that. How did the photoshoot go?"

Sawyer grinned. "We finished it last night. Grey will love it."

23

YEO AND CADEN

Yeo patted Auggie's back and swayed back and forth in his bedroom. He had agreed to watch Auggie for a few hours while Grey and Harper went to have lunch at The Irish Rose. Well, technically, Caden had agreed to watch the baby, but Yeo hadn't given him the chance.

He had Jackson on speakerphone, and he wanted to reach through the phone and shake his brother. "Jackson, I know something is upsetting you. Just tell me!"

His brother groaned. "Why are you so nosy?"

"Don't make me call Papa."

"You wouldn't." Jackson's voice sounded doubtful.

"Don't try me, little brother."

Jackson sighed. "There's this alpha..."

Yeo covered his mouth, muffling his squeal, and danced around the room. After a second, he paused and took a breath. "And?"

"You remember me telling you about Luke?"

Yeo frowned. "Yeah. You and Griff hang with him all the time. Have you talked him into asking Britney out yet?"

"Yeah, they're officially dating." Yeo's brother hesitated a moment. "It's just that talking with him made me realize some stuff about myself. I think I'm in love. Maybe. I don't know."

"In love? Jackson, what are you saying?"

"Nothing," Jackson said, voice getting high. "I'm not saying anything else. It's not important because this alpha and I would never work. He's not even interested in guys. Well, at least I don't think he is. He never talks about dating. He just listens to me bitch and moan."

Yeo sat on the end of the bed. "You're in love with him?"

"It doesn't matter," Jackson said. Yeo could hear people chattering in the background. "I have to get back to work, Yeo. Keep your mouth shut and don't say anything to Papa, okay?"

"I promise." Yeo hung up and bounced Auggie in his arms. "Jackson is in love with some alpha, Auggie. I think we need to keep our eyes and ears open. You'll tell me if you hear anything, right?"

Auggie smiled and grunted.

"You're such a good boy," Yeo said and left the bedroom. He walked down the hall and watched his husband for a moment. Caden worked on his laptop on the couch, face focused and intense.

"I can feel you staring, angel." Caden didn't look up, but his lips twitched.

Yeo sniffed the baby's head and sighed. His baby fever was back, and it was hitting him hard. "We need another baby."

Caden looked up from his computer. "Nari isn't quite potty-trained yet, angel. Shouldn't we wait another year?"

Yeo turned to watch Nari play with Huckleberry. Their daughter banged around on the toy kitchen while

Huckleberry perched beside her. The rabbit wore a chef hat left over from last night's photoshoot.

Linc's favorite book by Grey was about a little boy who wanted to become a chef. He had all sorts of animal friends that were determined to help him, even though they ended up ruining everything. In the end, the little boy learned to appreciate his friends, and all the little animals learned to step back and let their human friend take the lead.

Of course, Linc had dressed as the little boy. Nari had worn the cutest little butterfly costume, and Summer had been a raccoon. Yeo's teenage sister had actually enjoyed herself. Even Yeo's step-mother, Fawn, had helped them arrange everything, but she had drawn the line at donning a costume herself.

Huckleberry had made a convincing rabbit while Sassy, their little dog, had worn her mouse costume with pride. Well, until Magnolia started chasing her around. Yeo's big Maine Coon was a bit of a hunter, even when dressed as a humming bird.

"By the time the baby gets here, Nari will be potty-trained," Yeo said. "She's catching on a lot quicker than Linc did."

Caden grinned. "She hasn't used the litterbox at all."

"Don't give her ideas." Yeo made a face. "Anyway, Jackson has pretty much taken over the daily duties of the bookstore, and Amy and my two part-timers are doing well. It would be a good time for another baby."

"Maybe you should stop sniffing Auggie," Caden said, eyes twinkling.

Yeo stuck his tongue out. "You can't make me."

Caden reached out and pulled Yeo down on the couch. "I'll give you as many babies as I can, angel. Well, up to five. After that, you'll have to convince me."

Yeo cuddled Auggie to his chest and leaned into Caden's side. His alpha was a big pushover. He'd give Yeo anything he wanted. "Would you really mind another baby so quickly? You know I want a houseful. Somehow Papa managed it, and you and I are much better prepared than he was. We even have two empty rooms."

Caden looked thoughtful. "I work from home, and you work just downstairs. Linc is starting school soon, and I guess Nari *will* be potty-trained. Probably. Okay, let's do it."

Yeo smirked. No more birth control for them, and soon enough, he'd have an Auggie of his own. With his luck, he'd have the opposite of Augge – a demon baby. Oh well. He'd still love them.

Caden's phone dinged with a text, and his alpha read over it, frowning.

"What's wrong?" Yeo asked.

"You remember Cain's client? The one he was worried about when he was up for Halloween?"

Yeo bit his lip. "Yeah. The omega whose ex's new husband tried to hire someone to kill him."

Caden's face look grim. "Cain says the man just found the brakes on his car cut."

"Seriously? That's horrible. I assume it was the ex's new omega?"

Caden shrugged. "Cain seems convinced it is, but apparently, law enforcement won't take the man's threat seriously. They say he was just joking."

Yeo growled. "Why are people so stupid?"

Caden kissed his cheek. "The police probably see things like this all the time. Cain says the asshole can tell a good lie."

Yeo huffed. "Good-looking smooth talkers suck donkey balls."

Caden eyed him suspiciously. "Have you been hanging out with Abel?"

Yeo chuckled. "He's *your* best friend. It's kind of hard to avoid him."

"Speaking of best friends, we better get ready before we're late meeting Bennett," Caden said.

Yeo stood. "Auggie and I are ready. We're waiting on you, Roxanne Baxter."

Caden blushed. "Sorry. I got caught up in a scene."

Yeo narrowed his eyes. "What's happening to Josh and Lonnie? You can tell me, honey bunches. I can keep a secret."

Caden picked up Nari and tossed her in the air, laughing at her giggles. "I'm not telling your papa a thing about my story. He can read it when it releases."

Yeo scowled. "Why did I marry you again?"

Caden gave him a hot look, then headed for the door. "You love me, angel. It can't be helped."

"Are we sure Griff isn't dating Luke Jennings," Caden said, scowling. The fucker better watch out if he hurt Justin's brother.

Nari watched him closely, then turned toward the couple a few booths over and glared too, her hands propped on her hips.

Yeo shared an amused look with Bennett. "We're sure. They're just good friends. Sheesh."

Bennett leaned forward, and his youngest son, Nate, mimicked him, putting his chin on his little fist. "I hear that this is Luke's fourth date with Britney. Apparently, Britney's grandmother thinks it's love."

"It's just four dates," Caden said, shrugging. Oh, wait. He'd fallen in love with Yeo before they even managed one date.

Yeo arched an eyebrow, and Caden blushed. "No room to judge there, big guy."

"True."

"Nari, play," Nate said, holding his arms out.

Caden laughed and handed Nari over the table to Bennett. The two toddlers hugged each other and plopped their butts onto the booth. Nari showed her best friend the new knitted rabbit hat Ernie had made her. Nate was a little older than Caden's daughter, but he loved spending time with her.

Bennett watched them fondly. "Do you think these two will be best friends when they're older?"

Yeo grinned. "They'll be Nate and Nari forever."

Zoe scowled as she sat beside Bennett. "Hey, guys. I'm going to pretend Caden doesn't have Huckleberry strapped to his chest *in a bakery* where no pets are allowed. Jayla will bring your order out in a minute."

Caden winced and petted Huckleberry's long ears. Huck was a people rabbit. He insisted on going where his people went.

Bennett wrapped an arm around her. "What's wrong with you, baby girl? You aren't usually so scowly."

She settled her head on her uncle's shoulder. "Things."

Caden had a feeling he knew what bothered her. Mrs. Bethel had practically glared at him when he crossed paths with her at the grocery store yesterday, and he was just an honorary Wilson. The woman was not pleased her alpha son was marrying a beta, little less a Wilson.

Bennett looked sad. "I remember the Bethels always

made a huge deal out of Christmas, even after Gib's dad passed away."

"It's breaking Gib's heart," Zoe said. "He loves his mom and misses all the traditions they had. He even offered to share his family's pecan pie recipe with me, but it doesn't feel right. I know she hates me."

"Daphne Bethel is an idiot, and she'll realize it one day," Bennett said.

Zoe kissed Bennett's cheek, then reached out and took Auggie from Yeo. "I'll figure it out. Look at Luke and Britney. Aren't they adorable?"

Caden scowled again. "Is Griff really okay with that? What about Jackson? They both spend a lot of time with Luke."

Zoe gave him dry look. "They're both fine with Luke dating Britney. Calm down, big tough alpha man."

Bennett tapped his chin, and Nate mimicked him again, his round face solemn. "Now, if it was a different man dating Britney, it would be another story for Jackson."

Zoe gasped. "What do you know, Uncle Bennett? Tell us!"

Bennett shrugged. "I noticed at the Halloween party that Jackson *admired* a certain alpha's rear end. Several times."

Caden tilted his head, confused. "So? Jackson is a healthy young man. It's not surprising that he'd check someone out."

Bennett grinned. "This someone is one of Jackson's best friends. I've never seen Jackson look at him that way before. I would bet you anything that Jackson has some strong feelings for the man. He may go on about not trusting any alpha, but he trusts this alpha."

Caden felt Yeo's eyes on him, so he turned to look at his omega. His dark eyes were full of love and adoration.

"I never thought I'd trust another alpha after growing up the way I did, but the right man came along and convinced my heart to take a chance," Yeo said. "It was the best thing that ever happened to me."

"Aww," Zoe said, a sweet look on her face. "You two are so adorable I could puke. You really should talk to Jackson, Yeo. No one should miss out on love because they're afraid to take a risk."

Caden squeezed Yeo's hand. Meeting his angel had brought him so much joy. He really hoped Jackson found his own angel.

"I have talked with him a bit," Yeo said, surprising Caden. "Let's just say that my darling Bennett here is right."

Zoe's eyes widened and she bounced. "Who is it, Yeo? Tell me."

"Yeah, angel. Tell us," Caden added.

Yeo gave them all a smug look. "It's not my secret to tell." His smile turned into a scowl. "Plus, I don't know who it is."

Zoe hissed at him until Bennett smacked her arm. "Our food's coming. Behave, Zoe Lawson."

Jayla smiled as she set their tray of cinnamon rolls in the center of the table. "Here you go!"

"Cimis!" Nate and Nari both called out, standing back up in the booth.

Jayla laughed, then looked around. "Where's Linc? He likes his cimis too."

Caden tore apart a cinnamon roll on a small plate, then set it in front of the two toddlers. They liked sharing their food, and neither of them needed more than half a cinnamon roll.

"Linc is at Abuela's with his bestie," Yeo said, taking a bite of his own treat.

Jayla nodded. "I should have known. Linc and Iggy don't like to be apart."

Zoe's bit her lip, trying to hide a smile. "You know us Wilsons start young, right? Elijah and I knew we were going to be best friends when we were babies. All the Wilson littles are doing the same thing."

Caden liked that idea. He may have had good parents and two brothers, but somehow, Caden had still been lonely growing up. Looking back, he knew each member of the family should have made more of an effort with one another. He was closer to his family now then he had ever been.

As if his thoughts summoned him, Caden saw his father through the bakery window. John Benson saw him and grinned before coming in.

Nari squealed when she saw her grandad. "Paw paw!"

John reached over and grabbed his granddaughter. "Son, you aren't supposed to have your rabbit in the bakery."

Caden scowled and took a bite of his cinnamon roll, ignoring Yeo and Zoe's laughs.

Nate whined and held his arms out towards John, so Caden's dad settled Nari on one hip and reached for Nate with his empty arm. "You want to stay with Nari, don't you? I have my eye on you, Nate Wilson."

Nate giggled and kissed his cheek. "Love Nari."

John huffed. "You darn charming Wilsons."

24

BENNETT AND MARCO

Bennett left the bakery with a sugar high, and Nate bounced in his arms, chattering away. Bennett stroked his son's back and walked to Shawn's garage a few streets over. Shawn and the garage's former manager had bought out the owner last week. The paperwork was still processing, but it was a done deal.

Shawn and George stood outside the shop, watching Tomás and Juan hang the new sign with the words *Hobson Hills Garage* printed in large, blue letters.

"My son the businessman," Bennett said, clapping. Nate clapped too, giggling as the poof on the top of his knitted cap bounced.

Shawn grinned and pulled Nate into his arms. "Hey, little man. Do you like the sign, Papa? Tomás made it."

Bennett went and held the bottom of Tomás' ladder as the young man worked. He knew his adopted son was safe enough, but it made him nervous seeing him up that high. "You did a good job, Tomás. It looks great."

Tomás flushed and grinned down at Bennett. "Thanks, Papa. Oh yeah, before I forget, I'm supposed to tell you that

Ernie finished the costumes for our photo shoot tonight. I brought them to your house."

"Thank you, sweetheart," Bennett said. "You two be careful."

"I'll keep him safe, Bennett," Juan said, laughing.

Bennett stuck his tongue out at Juan, then turned back to Shawn and George. "Do you need any help with the party?"

Shawn and George were hosting a grand opening of sorts on Saturday. The shop had only changed names, but they wanted to do something special for the occasion. Bennett's nephew Abel was providing food from his pub, Zoe was bringing baked goods, and Bennett's brother-in-law Barry was hosting events in the parking lot for the day.

"Nope," Shawn said, handing Nate back to Bennett. "Everything's covered. Sometimes it pays to have a big family."

Bennett snorted. "Only sometimes. Jackson was complaining that everyone was being nosy about Luke Jennings."

Juan yelped as he almost dropped the sign he was holding up. "Jackson and Luke are a thing? They've been spending a lot of time together lately, but I didn't think it was like that."

Bennett raised an eyebrow. "They're just friends, Juan. Luke is dating someone now, and Jackson is happy for them."

Juan stared hard at the sign in his hand. "That's good."

"Poor Luke," Shawn said, laughing. "I bet everyone is in his business."

Bennett kept his eyes on Juan. "Of course. Well, I'll let you all get back to work. See you later tonight." Bennett left them and drove toward Ernie's house. "Nate, I think Juan and Jackson need a little Wilson push to figure things out."

"Nari pretty." His youngest had a one-track mind.

"She is pretty, baby boy." Bennett shook his head and laughed. Wilsons really did start young.

He parked in the garage, then let Nate out of his car seat. Oggy and Pickles met them at the door. "I brought your baby home, Pickles. Don't worry."

The calico cat glared at him, then wound around Nate. The little boy plopped onto the floor and pet the cat. "Kitty good."

Oggy waited patiently for Bennett's attention. He knelt and pet the large Saint Bernard. "Did you guard the house, Oggy boy?"

"Chicky time!" Nate said, standing back up and wiggling.

"He's bossy, Oggy," Bennett whispered into his dog's ear. "Okay, Nate. Let's go check on Margie and the chickens."

Oggy followed them outside and walked with them through the thick snow. The other animals were too happy inside the warm house to join them.

There were two barns on the property. The largest was meant for injured cattle or heifers close to calving. The smaller one held their horses and Bennett's cow, Margie. The chickens had a large coop and run behind the small barn.

"Daddy!" Nate let go of Bennett's hand and ran toward the chicken coop.

Marco stood next to the coop with an egg basket. He winced when Nate tripped and fell face-first into the snow.

Their son looked up, face grumpy. "Poo-poo!"

Marco started laughing and the chickens startled, squawking their displeasure.

"Stop laughing," Bennett said, trying to hide his own giggles. "What are you doing home already?"

Marco wiped his eyes, still chuckling. "Dean and I checked on a few of the new calves. I thought I'd take care of your cow and chickens for you."

Bennett smiled and kissed his cheek. "Thank you. Nate and I can go get you some coffee."

Marco kissed him gently on the lips. "I still have some in my thermos. No sense in walking back and forth."

Bennett handed Nate to his daddy and jumped up to perch on the railing of the coop. He watched Marco and Nate talk to the chickens and gather the few eggs. Chickens weren't too keen on laying in the winter, but Marco had built a nice warm coop, so Bennett's chickens were a little more productive.

Damn, his alpha looked good. The grey in his hair was a little thicker this year and his waist wasn't quite so firm as it used to be, but Marco made it all look good. His husband's broad shoulders still carried the world for Bennett, and his smile still made Bennett's heart beat too fast.

Marco caught his eye and gave him a knowing grin. "Tali and I are going to take a ride before dinner. That okay?"

Bennett blew him a kiss. "Sure. Hannah has an English paper due tomorrow, and Drew is going to help her proofread it. I'll help Terry with their homework. Just be home by six."

Marco leaned up and kissed him again. "Yes, sir."

MARCO WATCHED Tali from the corner of his eye. His girl had something to say but was taking her sweet time about it.

The earflaps of Tali's warm hat bounced as they rode

their horses along their favorite path. The teenager was warmly dressed in jeans, boots, and a pink and grey coat. Marco could almost see the stress drain from her the longer they rode through the quiet woods.

"Dad?"

Marco grinned. Finally. "Yeah?"

"I... I need to ask you something." Tali's dark face was full of worry. "Promise you'll be honest?"

Marco nodded. "I will, Tali. What's wrong?"

"I'm ready for hormone replacement therapy. I've thought a lot about it, and I'll get an afterschool job and start saving up money."

Marco frowned. Tali helped him with the ranch after school. It was their thing.

"I thought that since I'm not going to college, maybe you and Papa could pay for some of it?" She winced. "If not, that's okay. I can save up until I can afford it."

Marco felt a ball of worry leave him. Bennett and he had expected and planned for this. He was just happy Tali hadn't been upset over her friend Tommy. He kept waiting on her to announce that the two of them were dating, and he didn't know how he felt about that.

"If you're ready, Bennett and I already researched the process and set aside the money," Marco said. "We've been talking with a really nice psychologist that can walk you through the mental health evaluation, and he recommended an endocrinologist."

Tali stopped her horse and looked at him, eyes wet with tears. "You already... I can really do it? It's so hard, Dad. I know you all love me, but I can't stand it sometimes. It's like I'm wearing someone else's body. I can *feel* my breasts missing. I know where my body is supposed to curve and it just doesn't. It's like I'm deformed and broken."

Macro reached over and took her hand, wishing he could hug her. "Tali, we'll get you an appointment made with Dr. Lyles. The way you feel is completely valid. You're a beautiful young lady, and we want you to be comfortable with yourself. We love you, Tali, and we'll always be there for you."

She wiped the tears from her cheeks and nodded. "I love you too, Dad."

They rode and talked for another hour before brushing the horses down and giving them some oats.

Bennett and Nate waited for them on the porch. "Are you two hungry yet? I think Nate may eat Drew."

"Oh no," Tali said, laughing. She scooped up the little boy and tossed him in the air. "You can't eat your brother, Nate."

Nate growled. "Hungry."

Marco pulled Bennett into his arms and kissed him. "Tali is ready for HRT."

Bennett grinned. "Finally. I know we decided not to push her, but I was starting to worry. I'll make an appointment with Dr. Lyles tomorrow."

Shawn and Tomás showed up right after Marco, so they all ate dinner, joking and laughing about school and work. After Drew and Terry washed dishes, they all dressed in their costumes.

"I feel kinda stupid," Drew said, pulling at the back of his tights. "What the heck am I wearing?"

Terry whacked him on the head with a plastic sword. They were dressed as a palace soldier. "You're a prince, so stop pulling your pants out of your butt. It's not princely."

Hannah and Tali giggled, heads pressed together. They were dressed as princesses and were trying to get Choco, Hannah's dog, into a goat costume. Butterscotch, Hannah's hamster, perched on her shoulder. The poor thing was getting up there in age, but still as active as ever.

"Here, I'll show you how to do it," Shawn said, kneeling in front of Choco. The young man was dressed as a king with a long, white beard.

In Marco's favorite story by Grey, two princesses compete with each other for the attention of a handsome prince. After plenty of shenanigans, the princesses, the prince, and the prince's best friend decide they'd much rather go on adventures together than get married.

It was one of Grey's books meant for older children, but Marco adored it. He wished Grey's books had been around when he was a kid.

He looked up from tying the goblin costume onto Honey, his ranch dog. Bennett led Nate and Oggy into the room. They were both dressed as trolls.

Pickles slinked in, glaring at them. The calico cat was dressed as a dragon, tail swishing back and forth. Tomás followed, watching the cat carefully. "Pickles did *not* want to wear the costume."

Terry grinned at him. "Aww, Tomás, you make a nice troll king."

Tomás grinned and picked up Nate. "My loyal subject!"

"Where's Frankie?" Hannah asked, looking around the room.

The white, fluffy cat came through the door. She wore a tiny crown of flowers on her head and a set of fairy wings.

Drew bowed deeply. "The Fairy Queen comes."

Nate giggled and clapped his hands.

Bennett laughed. "Alright. Let's get started. Our goal is to show Grey how awesome this story is, so get to work."

Marco sighed happily and took pictures of his huge, chaotic family.

25

DEAN AND RAY

Dean put the unicorn hat back on Beau. His golden retriever shook his head, and the hat fell to the floor of the barn. "Beau, come on. We need a unicorn."

Ray's deep laugh sent a shiver up Dean's back. Damn, he loved his man. "Jackie would be a good unicorn."

Dean looked over his shoulder. "You just want your donkey to steal the show."

Min ran past them, giggling. The little boy was dressed as a flower. Three miniature pigs chased him, all wearing fairy costumes.

Ray bounced their youngest, Jun, in his arms. The baby chewed on his fist and was also dressed as a flower. "Are you kidding? Min and Jun will steal the show."

"Dad, I don't want to be the mermaid," Jake said, voice plaintive. "Why can't Jules wear the tail?"

Dean smothered his laughter. Jake took baby steps, legs pulled tight together with a green shimmery tail. His blond wig was askew on his head, and his face wore a scowl somewhere beneath the thick makeup.

Dean couldn't hold it in. He bent at the waist, laughing hard. Jake just looked so grumpy.

"I can't be the mermaid," Jules said, carrying his cat, Pounce, into the barn. "Pounce and I are frogs."

Dean's favorite story of Grey's was about a little girl that got lost in a forest full of magical creatures. He had borrowed Olive for the morning to be their little girl. She loved this story even more than Dean and his kids did, so she hadn't been hard to convince.

Olive grinned widely and bounced behind Jules, Dean's guinea pig, Bonny, following behind her in a guinea pig ball. "Jake, you look beautiful!"

Jake scowled and waddled over to the rock where his beagle sat wearing her own mermaid costume. "Grey better appreciate this."

Dean started laughing again. "You are the grumpiest mermaid I've ever seen."

Jules gasped and set Pounce down. "That could be Grey's newest book – The Grumpiest Mermaid."

Dean laughed harder, leaning against Ray until his phone dinged. He looked at the text full of images. "Jimmy and his friends at school dressed like the group of talking trees and took pictures for us to add to our album. Dang, his friend Lona did a good job with the costumes."

Ray looked at his phone and grinned. "I love that boy."

"He's a young man," Dean reminded Ray.

"Don't remind me."

"Can we get a move on here?" Jake pouted. "I want out of this costume as soon as possible."

"I have the last of the fairies," Min-Jun said, coming from the back of the barn with his two cats, Betty and Lucy. They looked especially lovely in their fairy costumes.

Dean chuckled. "Everyone, take your places. Papa, will

you get Beau to keep his unicorn hat on? Where's El Paso? We can't have a magical forest without our troll."

A few hours later, Dean had a ton of pictures and Jackie the donkey was the official unicorn. Beau had decided he would just help Dean and Ray take pictures.

"Good job, everyone. Let's get some lunch."

Jake pulled the mermaid skirt off and ran toward the house in his underwear.

Dean looked at Ray. "He's your son when he does things like that."

"There's three inches of snow out there," Ray said, shaking his head. "Jules, will you take Jun on to the house? I'll help your papa put everything away."

"Okay." Jules put the baby on his hip. "You too, Mini-boo. I'll read you a story, okay?"

"Bear story?" Min watched his brother with big eyes. "Please?"

"I love that one," Olive said, picking Min up and spinning him. "Mr. Ray made cookies too. Stories and cookies are the best."

Dean smiled when they ran from the barn. He started undressing the animals and putting the costumes into a bag. It took him a minute to notice his papa was helping Ray and him.

"Papa, don't you have to get ready for your date?"

Min-Jun blushed. "I have a little time."

"Are you going to tell us who you've been dating the last two weeks?" Dean loved watching his papa flush from the teasing. Min-Jun had been seeing someone almost every night for two weeks. He was smitten, and it was fucking adorable.

"We'll be going together to Rue's birthday party this weekend, nosy." Min-Jun handed him the costume bag. "I think I'll go soak in the bathtub for an hour before my date."

Ray laughed. "You tell him, Min-Jun. It's none of our business."

Dean kissed his papa's cheek. "Have a good soak. Love you, Papa."

"Love you too."

AFTER LUNCH, Ray swayed slowly, arms around his omega. Dean's head was settled against his chest as they danced in the kitchen. The kids were decorating the photo album in the living room, and Ray was enjoying the quiet moment. The snow fell slowly outside the window, but it was warm and cozy in their home.

"What do you get when you cross a snowman and a vampire?" He kissed Dean's head and stroked a hand down his back.

Dean laughed and dug his fingers into Ray's shoulder. "What?"

"Frostbite."

Dean's laughter filled the room and heat filled Ray. He loved it when his omega smiled and laughed. He was meant for laughter.

"Ray, who do you think Papa is dating?"

Ray smiled into Dean's hair. "I think it really isn't any of our business."

"What if he's a horrible person? What if he's just like my dad?"

Ray thought for a moment. "He can't be. Min-Jun smiles too much for it to be a man like your dad."

Dean sighed and pressed his face against Ray. "I just

worry about him. Hobson Hills isn't that big, so I wonder who it is."

Ray thought for a moment. "Most of the men Min-Jun's age are married already. I guess Sheriff McKenzie is about his age and single. His omega passed away about ten years ago. At least that's what Tanner told me. Then there's the owner of the hardware store, Benjamin Cordell. He seems like a nice guy."

"It could be someone younger," Dean said, eyes dancing. "Younger men have more stamina."

Ray laughed and bent to kiss his husband. Dean's familiar taste made him shudder, and it didn't take long for him to want more. He pulled Dean down the hallway, pausing to peek in on the kids.

Poor Beau and Lola were covered in glitter, and Olive stood above the boys, Jun in her arms. She watched them work with a close eye. "Min, that's perfect. Will you help Jules and Beau with their page? Jake, Lola's paw prints are great, but those colors don't go together. Maybe use the blue and green glitter to bring it all together?"

Jake grinned over his shoulder. "Yes, ma'am."

Ray bit his lip to hold in his laughter and tugged Dean into their bedroom, shutting and locking the door behind him.

Dean pulled him down for another kiss and slid his hands under Ray's shirt to slide them across Ray's stomach and chest.

Ray pulled his shirt off and picked Dean up, carrying him to the bed. "Love you, cowboy."

Dean smiled softly, eyes full of warmth. "Love you too, hero. Come here." He pulled Ray down and kissed him.

Ray ran his hands up and down Dean's back, enjoying the feel of the hard muscles his cowboy carried. He especially loved his omega's firm ass. He reached for the lube and nuzzled his face against Dean's neck, slowly stroking his omega's dick.

Dean arched his hips and spread his legs wide. "I love it when you touch me."

Ray hummed and stretched Dean's hole with a lubed finger. "Probably not as much as I love touching you."

When he was stretched, Ray positioned himself and slowly entered Dean. His omega moaned and lifted his hips, wrapping his legs around Ray's waist. They moved together, and Ray gritted his teeth, the tightness around his dick driving him to move faster.

When he came, he felt Dean's cum splatter against his stomach. "Fuck, Dean." He panted. "The things you do to me."

Dean smiled and pulled him close. "My sweet beta."

They only had a few minutes of peace before Jake knocked on the door. "Papa, I think we're done. Come look."

They pulled apart, then hurriedly wiped down and dressed. Ray jumped when Dean smacked his butt. "Move it, hero."

"Like my ass, do you?"

Dean waggled his eyebrows. "Oh yeah. Hey, if you were ground coffee, you'd be Espresso 'cause you're so fine."

Ray laughed so hard he snorted. "What the hell was that?"

Dean chuckled. "Noah's trying out pick-up lines." He gave Ray a sultry look. "I was wondering if you had an extra heart. Mine seems to have been stolen."

They were laughing when they got to the living room, and Jake gave them a curious look. "What's so funny?"

"Nothing," Dean said, shaking his head.

Jules sighed. "You two were kissing again, weren't you?"

He turned to Olive. "They do this all the time. It's so annoying."

Olive nodded. "Dad and Daddy do the same thing. Adults are weird."

Jake grinned and gave them a knowing look. "They really are."

26

JUSTIN AND TANNER

Justin watched Tanner from the doorway of the nursery. Justin and his friends had spent a lot of time putting together Rhonda's room. They had painted the walls a light green and covered one in 3D butterfly decals. His mom's snow globes were displayed on a white shelf above the changing table, and a bookshelf full of Grey's books stood next to a comfortable rocking chair.

Grey's husband, Harper, had insisted on making all of the furniture. Justin still didn't understand how Harper could forgive him for being such a jerk for years. It felt odd accepting gifts from him even though Grey and Justin were best friends. Hell, it still felt odd to have friends.

Justin shook himself and watched his alpha gently rock their newborn daughter who was currently bundled up in a wombat costume. Tanner's eyes were full of absolute wonder. He had barely set Rhonda down since she was born, and it was sweet, but also kind of annoying.

"Are you almost ready?" Justin bit his lip, fighting laughter, when Tanner jumped.

Tanner grinned sheepishly. "Yeah. Sorry. I get lost watching her sometimes. Isn't she the most beautiful thing you've ever seen?"

Justin pressed his lips together, amused. "You have changed her diapers, right? That was you who got up to feed her three times last night?"

Tanner made a face. "You're just as bad as me. You were relieved when I had to start back to work."

Justin snorted. "It was the only way I got to hold our daughter."

Tanner chuckled. "You make a good point."

Buttons, their guinea pig, rolled through Justin's legs in his ball. "Are you ready to go? Buttons here thinks you're dragging your feet."

Tanner groaned. "I don't want to wear a costume. All the other families are just dressing up the kids and pets."

"We only have two pets and one baby."

Tanner arched an eyebrow. "You say that like it's a bad thing."

Justin laughed. "Compared to the rest of the Wilsons, it is."

"You two are holding up the photoshoot," Griff called from the living room. "Laura just texted me to drag your butts downstairs."

Justin felt a little hand on the side of his leg and looked down. His niece, Bea, watched him with big blue eyes. The little girl wore a koala costume, and her dark hair was styled into two buns on top of her head.

She chewed on her fist and gave him a sloppy smile. "I go up?"

Justin smiled and picked her up. Ever since Griff had moved to Hobson Hills, Justin had gotten to spend a lot of time with his brother and his niece. "How's it going, honey bee?"

"Want yum-yum."

Tanner laughed and leaned over to kiss the giggling girl's cheek. "You're always hungry, Bebe."

Bea leaned over and puckered her lips. "Kiss Ronnie."

Tanner held the baby up and let Bea kiss her head. "Ronnie loves your kisses."

Griff leaned around Justin. "Guys, really. Come on before Laura comes up here and drags us all downstairs. The woman is scary."

Justin nodded. Laura *was* scary. "Let's go. We still need to dress up."

"North brought the costumes." Griff reached down and grabbed Button's ball. "Nell already grabbed Butter Bunny too."

Justin pulled Tanner through the house and followed Griff downstairs. Bea's favorite book by Grey was about a ranch in Australia. She loved all the different animals and would spend hours with Justin reading the book over and over.

Justin could understand why Grey was worried about taking a chance with his books. As bright and kind as the omega was, he was also a little insecure. Just like Justin.

They went to the dining room of The Irish Rose. It was early enough that the pub hadn't opened yet, but all the staff had gathered with their families for the photoshoot. Laura was dressed as a rancher and her kids were little wombats like Rhonda. Others were dressed as cattle dogs, house cats, kangaroos, horses, cows, koalas, wombats, and crocodiles. There was even a little Tasmanian devil.

"Please tell me we get to be ranchers too," Tanner said, sighing.

Laura smirked. "There are only three humans in the story, Tanner, and Griff, Justin, and I have them covered."

Justin's eldest brother, Zed, stepped forward, and he started laughing. The big alpha was dressed like a kangaroo and Butter Bunny rode in his pouch.

Zed handed Tanner a bulky costume. "You're another kangaroo, man. Deal with it."

A FEW HOURS LATER, Tanner finally got to shuck the kangaroo costume and managed to again find his dignity. It had helped to have Zed hopping around the pub with him, but still, the things he did for Justin.

By the time he made it back downstairs, the pub was open, and Justin had grabbed them a table against the window. Tanner watched his omega from the bar.

Justin smiled, then laughed at something Griff said. His eyes were bright and happy. *Damn, I'm a lucky man.*

Mateo set a pint of beer in front of a customer, then slid over to him. "You going to join them?"

Tanner didn't look away from Justin. "Yeah. I'm just admiring my husband."

Mateo slapped his back. "We are lucky bastards, you and I."

Tanner shot him a look. "How did your own photoshoot go today?"

The large man winced. "Abel's dads and Iggy's grandparents were there. I don't think it was a good idea to introduce them. I think they're planning themed holiday photoshoots now."

Tanner laughed, but he felt a little jealous. He wasn't too close to his own parents, and they didn't really like Justin.

They hadn't even seemed interested in meeting Rhonda. His mom had told him to get a blood test to make sure the baby was his. She honestly thought Justin had wanted to trick Tanner into marrying him.

"By the way," Mateo said. "Gramps and Grammy aren't too pleased that Zed hasn't made it to a Sunday breakfast yet. You might want to give him fair warning. I think Gramps is planning on *visiting* him next week."

Tanner rubbed his chin. "Zed isn't shy exactly, but he likes his own company. Does that make sense?"

Mateo shrugged. "Tell that to Gramps. The man is determined to join your family to his."

"I think he just likes Bea," Tanner said, chuckling.

"That is entirely possible."

A customer called for Mateo, and Tanner left the bar. He sat next to Justin, taking a moment to kiss his husband's cheek.

Justin smiled at him, then turned back to Zed. "I'm just saying that I know some omegas who would love to spend some time with you. There's no reason to spend your nights cooped up in your house."

Griff shook his head, eyes worried. "You don't even have a pet, Zed."

Zed snuggled Rhonda. "You two don't need to worry. I'm doing alright without dating or a pet. I have my houseplant. Don't forget Eugenia."

Griff rolled his eyes. "How can I forget? I had to keep that damn fern alive while you were overseas. You are way too attached to that thing."

Zed kissed Rhonda's head. "I also have Bea and Ronnie. Let me savor being an uncle, guys."

Tanner hid a smile. There was no way Griff and Justin would let Zed be alone. There would be some kind of pet keeping the alpha company soon enough. Then there was Gramps and the rest of the Wilsons. Yeah, Zed was out of luck.

Movement over by the window caught his eye. "Isn't that Luke? Griff, I thought you were dating him?"

Griff groaned and banged his head on the table, making Bea laugh. "I swear, small towns are ridiculous. Luke and I are just friends."

Zed's eyes narrowed on the couple across the room. "The asshole doesn't know what he's missing. You're ten times better than that woman."

"You're a nurse," Tanner said, nodding. "You help people every day and make being a single parent look easy. Luke would be lucky to have you." Tanner was proud of Griff. The man had grown up dirt poor, just like Justin, and had worked hard to make something of himself. He took good care of Bea too.

Justin laughed. "Get used to gossip, Griff. Nell told me someone told her that Luke, Jackson, and you were a throuple."

Griff moaned and looked up at the ceiling. "If only my life was half as exciting as everyone thinks it is."

Tanner laughed as the brothers started squabbling about dating, ferns, and gossip. He should probably miss his parents, but these three men and two children were his family now, and he already felt closer to Zed and Griff than he did to the people who raised him. His mom and dad didn't know what they were missing out on.

27

ABEL AND MATEO

bel turned his blinker on, then switched lanes. Traffic had slowed down quite a bit since they'd left the airport. It should only take a couple of hours to get home, but with the frequent pee breaks he would be taking thanks to the baby girl sitting on his bladder, it would probably be more like three.

Gabriela and Fernando were going to spend the winter break with them, and Abel was looking forward to it. Now, though, it was time to focus on the interrogation. He needed to ease into it or Gabriela's new boyfriend might jump from the car. He glanced at Valentina in the front seat.

She nodded at him before looking into the back seat. "So, Artie, what's your major?"

Abel watched the young man blink in confusion. *Uh oh.*

"I don't know. It's freshman year, so I haven't thought about it," Artie said. "I like music."

Abel gripped the steering wheel. Fuck trumpet. The next thing the boy said had best *not* be that he was in a band.

"My friends and I have a band," Artie said. "We play every Friday and Saturday at the Cumbubble."

Abel took a breath. "The Cumbubble?"

"It's a bar close to campus," Gabriela said, slapping Fernando when her brother started to laugh.

"A bar? You two are only eighteen. How is it possible for you to work in a bar, Artie?"

The young man shrugged. "The owner's really laid back. He doesn't ask our age, and we don't tell him."

Abel's lips clamped together, and he fought a scowl.

"Does your band play the sunshine song?" Iggy asked from the very back of the SUV. Linc and he sat close together, reading one of their favorite books. "Grey and Harper sing it to us all the time. It's the best."

Artie grinned over his shoulder. "Little dudes, I'll play you any song you want. I brought my guitar. We'll party all night."

Valentina cleared her throat. "That sounds fun and age appropriate. How are classes going, Artie?"

"Okay, I guess. They're really boring, and the college, like, makes you go to class. If you don't, they drop you. It's so stupid."

Abel almost whimpered. This was the guy Gabriela had said she'd fallen in love with?

"Wow. That must be so hard," Valentina said, voice dry. "Your grades are alright, though, since you have to go?"

"I don't know," Artie said. "I don't think they released grades yet."

"They have," Fernando said, glee in his voice. "Here, we can check yours on my phone."

"No, that's okay," Gabriela said quickly and smacked her brother again.

"Oh, please," Abel said. "Let's check his grades."

They weren't promising.

"I got a C," Artie said, surprised. "That's awesome."

"You also got two Ds and an F," Fernando said.

"Ds get degrees," Artie said, grinning.

Abel squeaked but managed to keep his mouth shut. Valentina's wide eyes watched him for a moment as she struggled not to laugh.

"I'm gonna be a policeman when I grow up," Linc said, smiling at Artie. "Tanner is a policeman, and he gets to wear a shiny badge. I'm gonna take Huckleberry with me, and we'll patrol the streets, keeping peoples safe, and both of us are gonna have shiny badges."

Fernando bit his lip, trying not to laugh. "Huckleberry is his pet rabbit."

Artie blinked at him. "That's, like, the best thing I've ever heard. You're going places, little dude."

If only Artie would go some other place, Abel thought, sighing.

A couple of hours later, they stopped to get gas and take a bathroom break. Valentina and Gabriela hunted for a bathroom while Fernando pumped gas.

Abel turned and looked at Artie. The young man had a scraggly beard and was a bit plain. His smile was nice, though, if a bit strained.

"Gabby's really nervous about me meeting her brother. Do you think he'll like me? I know I'm not, like, the best guy on campus, and she could do so much better than me. I love her though. She's so smart and funny. Did you know she made a club, and they do all kinds of smart things? Like, they started this garden, and we pick stuff from it and bring it to the homeless shelter. Who does stuff like that?"

Abel sighed. *Damn it.* "I think as long as you're honest with Mateo, he'll give you a chance. Gabriela is very special and you need to remember that. Start thinking about your future."

Artie blinked. "It's just freshmen year."

"Artie, don't make me jump back there and smother you with Fernando's duffle bag."

The young man's face wrinkled. "His bag stinks."

"I know," Abel said, nodding calmly.

"Okay. I'll, like, start thinking."

"Think about your abilities and what you're passionate about," Abel said. "Think of something that will get you employed."

"I like music," Artie said, rubbing his goatee. "Like, I could be a rock star."

"Employment," Abel said again, voice hard. "Think about employment."

Artie nodded, resembling a bobble head. "Yeah. What did you major in Mr. Lawson?"

Abel sighed. "Abel. My name is Abel. I majored in, uh, brewing."

Artie blinked again. "You can make money doing that?"

"If you're very good at it," Abel said, wincing. He may not be the best role model here. *Fuck, I'm an old man.*

"I'm going to be a teacher like Uncle Ernie and Uncle Fernando," Iggy said. "You could be a teacher too." He started bouncing in his seat. "You could be a music teacher."

Artie gave Abel a bright look. "Yeah, I could do that."

Abel gave the young man a hard look. "*You* need to figure it out. You can't rely on two children to plan your life for you."

Artie slumped into his seat. "Yes, sir."

MATEO MOVED AROUND THE KITCHEN, putting the finishing touches on the callaloo soup he was cooking for dinner. His omega would be home from the airport soon. "I should have taken off from work and gone to the airport myself."

Pete sipped his beer and scratched Gordo's ears. The fat English bulldog sat in the man's lap, relaxed and happy. "Abel's perfectly capable of driving a few hours, pregnant or not. He wanted to go, and if you'd tried to stop him, he'd have probably clobbered you with a beer stein."

Carol laughed. "My precious Abel wouldn't do that."

Really, Carol? Mateo thought. He knew the woman adored Abel, but the two had spent a lot of time together. Surely, she knew his husband was perfectly capable of beating him with a beer stein.

"He collects beer steins for the pub, you know," Carol said, shrugging. "He wouldn't risk damaging one."

Mateo snorted. "So true."

Pete smiled at his wife, then looked back to Mateo. "While we have you alone, we wanted to talk to you about something."

Carol reached across the table and scratched Gordo's head. "I know we're only technically related to Iggy, but we love you like a son, Mateo. Valentina may be your sister, but she feels like our granddaughter. I know the more we get to know Gabriela and Fernando, the more they'll feel like our own too."

Mateo turned away from the stove and gave them his full attention. "You have no idea how thankful I am that I met Doug and we had Iggy."

Carol smiled sadly. "We miss our son every day, but we're thankful he gave us you and Iggy. Now, you've given us even more."

"What we wanted to talk to you about was our place in

your family," Pete said. "Abel welcomed us with open arms, but is it too much to hope that we can be grandparents to Valentina and the new baby too?"

Mateo gave them a soft look. "You already are. Valentina calls you Grandpa and Grandma, and Abel and I fully expect Emma will too when she's born."

Carol wiped at her wet eyes. "Thank you. We love them all, Mateo, including you. We'll be by to visit often."

Pete cleared his throat and set Gordo on the floor. "We should get ready for dinner, honey. We're meeting Barry and Jamie at the diner in town."

"What? You don't want to meet Gabriela's boyfriend?"

Carol gave him an amused look. "Valentina has been texting me. I think we'll leave Artie to you."

The two left and Mateo finished dinner and cut up some crusty French bread he'd begged off Reuben. He heard the sound of Abel's new SUV in the driveway and hurried to set the table. His omega would be hungry. He always was.

Abel, Linc, and Iggy were the first ones inside, and all three went straight to the bathroom, only pausing to kiss his cheek before running. Linc's kiss was a little slobbery, and he wiped off his cheek.

Fernando came in next, eyes dancing with laughter. "You're going to love Artie, big brother. I promise." He laughed all the way to the guest room down the hall.

Mateo sighed and went outside to help with the luggage. A tall, thin, scraggly-looking teenager was kissing his sister. The asshole looked like the member of a grunge band. *I don't like him.*

An hour later, Mateo stared at Artie across the dinner table. *I really don't like him.* The kid was not good enough for Gabriela. He felt Abel's gentle kick, and he cleared his throat. "How did the interview with the school go, Fernando?"

His brother grinned. "As long as I pass my last semester, I have the job. The principal said middle school was like a trial by fire. If I survive the first three years, I'll be good."

Iggy looked up from his bowl, mouth full of bread. "Uncle Ernie likes teaching. He can show you how to do it right."

Linc nodded, looking extraordinarily wise for a four-year-old. "Ernie is super smart. He hunts Big Foot and almost caught him last week."

Artie's eyes brightened. "Really? You know Big Foot is an alien, right?"

Gabriela groaned and buried her face in her hands. "Artie, you're supposed to be impressing Mateo and Abel. Remember?"

Mateo frowned. "He's right, Gabriela. It's common knowledge Big Foot was left on Earth by an alien species. Why else would there be so many Big Foot and UFO sightings in the same places?"

Abel and the others stared at him, but Artie grinned. "Seriously. Big Foot's, like, their way of watching humans without drawing too much attention."

Mateo smiled. Maybe this kid wasn't as bad as he thought. "Yeah. You need to go with us on our next excursion, Artie. I've only been out once with Ernie, but he has a lot of gear. You'll love it."

"I'm so there, man," Artie said, nodding eagerly.

Abel cleared his throat. "Are your parents upset that you're spending the holidays away from home, Artie?"

The young man shook his head. "No. They're divorced. I don't see Dad much, and Mom's new husband doesn't like me."

Linc stopped eating and reached out to take Artie's hand. "You can visit us all the time. We like new friends, don't we Iggy?"

Mateo's son nodded so hard his glasses almost fell off. "We do. You can play with us, okay? We're going to play with Poppy and Pudding after dinner."

Gabriela smiled. "I don't know if Artie wants to play with a rabbit and a lizard, Iggy."

Iggy gave her an affronted look. "Pudding is a dragon, Aunt Gabby."

Artie gave him an excited look. "A dragon? That sounds awesome."

Fernando snickered when Gabriela rolled her eyes.

After dinner, Valentina and Mateo did dishes while Abel propped his feet up, hands resting on his big belly. Abel's Saint Bernard, Nana, lay on the floor beside him, while Gordo cleaned up the crumbs from under the table. Mateo's cat, Ragamuffin, watched him from a windowsill.

"What do you think of Artie?" Mateo asked his youngest sister.

Valentina shrugged. "He's not perfect, but he really cares about Gabriela and that's important."

Cupcake, Valentina's kitten, ran into the room and jumped on the table before launching herself across the room and onto Valentina's shoulder. Mateo's sister didn't even blink. This was their new normal.

Mateo scowled at the kitten and ignored its hiss. "What about you, Valentina? Are there any crushes I need to worry about?"

Valentina blushed and gave him a horrified look. "What are you talking about?"

Mateo swallowed hard. "I just want to make sure you know that you can tell me anything, hermanita. If you have any questions about sex or relationships, I'll be happy to answer them."

"Why would you... No... just no."

"I'm here for you, Valentina."

She tossed the dishrag in the sick and backed away, reaching up to steady the kitten on her shoulder. "I'm going to visit Grandpa and Grandma." She ran for the front door, and Mateo knew she was going to Carol and Pete's RV. Iggy's grandparents were parked in the back and plugged into the house.

"Do you think they're back from dinner?" Abel asked, struggling not to laugh.

Mateo shrugged. "I don't think she cares."

Abel started laughing. "No. Oh, donkey balls, did you see her face?"

Mateo winced. "Was it that bad?" He knelt beside Abel and pressed his hands to his omega's belly. It still amazed him that there was a little girl growing in there – a little girl he had helped create.

"Yes," Abel said, laughing harder. "I'll talk to her about it, handsome. Don't worry."

Mateo sighed when Gordo crawled into his lap. "I'm lucky to have you, mi alma."

Abel ran his fingers through Mateo's hair. "Don't you forget it. Now might be a good time to tell you that I invited Charlie and his brothers to the winter festival at the end of the month."

Mateo grumbled. "Fucking Charming Charlie."

28

ERNIE AND REUBEN

"I love my knitting room, Reuben, and I couldn't possibly give it up." Ernie finished buttoning Clover's ladybug onesie. They may have finished the photoshoot for Grey's book already, but he wasn't ready to give up the ladybug costumes. Clover and Tony looked adorable in them.

"Then we could put the kids all in one room," Reuben said, making a face as he struggled with Pudge's sweater. The puppy liked licking any bit of skin he could find and his tail wagged fast, whapping at Reuben's hands as he tried to avoid the puppy's tongue.

"That just doesn't work," Ernie said and patted his slightly rounded belly. "We'll already have two of them sharing a room, and we couldn't put all three in one room."

The upstairs Roomba quietly rolled across the floor. Sunny, Ernie's cat, sat on it. She was still dressed in her butterfly costume from the photoshoot and didn't seem to mind the fancy wings strapped to her back. Their other cat, Ahab, crouched beneath the twins' L-shaped crib, glaring his displeasure. He hadn't liked wearing his own costume.

"I don't want to share our bed with Big Foot," Reuben said, voice frustrated. "I can't believe we're arguing about this."

"I need to have a plan ready if we find him next week." Ernie patted Clover's belly and checked in on Tony one more time. His sweet boy was already asleep after his warm bottle and diaper change. "What if we find Big Foot and I bring him home, and we don't have anywhere to put him?"

Reuben rubbed his face. "Juan could take him home."

Ernie made a face. "Juan lives in an apartment. That's no place for Big Foot. Plus, I'm worried about Juan. He isn't in any condition to take care of Big Foot."

"Why would you have to bring him home at all?"

Ernie reminded himself to be patient. Sometimes Reuben just didn't understand things the way he ought to. "Big Foot lives alone in the woods. He's obviously lonely and needs love and attention."

Reuben gave him a frustrated look. "We could give him my cabin and go visit him every day. Would that work?"

Ernie pressed his hand to his heart. "Your cabin is your sanctuary."

Reuben cupped his face and kissed him. "You're my sanctuary, Ernie."

Ernie sniffled. "That's the sweetest thing you've ever said."

Reuben hugged him close and laughed softly. "You said that this morning when I told you I'd make you apple cider waffles."

"I was really hungry." Ernie hummed with pleasure just thinking about breakfast. "You always put fried apples on top of them."

Reuben kissed him again. "Now that the important question of where Big Foot will stay if you find him on your excursion next week is settled, Pudge and I are going to Grammy's house to help cook for Rue's birthday party."

"Niccolo's coming over to stay with the twins. He said he didn't feel up to going to the party." Ernie reluctantly let Reuben go. "I'll wrap up our album and check on the alpacas before coming."

"Tell Peppermint I love him."

Ernie rolled his eyes. "Yeah, yeah. I'll tell your alpaca that you love him." He watched Reuben and Pudge go, then looked back at Clover and Tony. "Your daddy really loves Peppermint, baby burritos."

The babies didn't care. They were sleeping and happy.

He went to his knitting room downstairs and looked at their photo album for Grey. Ernie's favorite story by Grey was about two ladybugs and their adventure crossing a meadow. It focused more on insects than some of his other stories, but that just made it more fun. He had never known ants could be so interesting.

He sighed happily and sat in his rocking chair. His knitting room was his haven. Juan and Carter had finished it three days ago, and Reuben had helped him move all his yarn and half-finished projects to their new home. The room was small but full of windows overlooking their newly fenced-in backyard.

He moved around the room, organizing his yarns, until Niccolo arrived. His friend had been recently injured and was finally cleared to drive short distances and carry his daughter, Eliza. Now he was trying to convince Grammy and Gramps that he should move out on his own. It wasn't working.

"Hey," Niccolo said, yawning. Eliza was sleeping in his arms. "I think I'm going to lay her down and check on the twins before taking my own nap."

"Are you alright?" Niccolo looked drained.

"I'm fine. The trial is getting closer, and I'm worried about it. I shouldn't be. All I have to do is show up and answer questions. I guess it's just facing Mr. Dennings. I thought he was my friend."

"I'm sorry, Nic."

Niccolo smiled. "Nothing to do about it. I'm going to enjoy a little down time and some babies. Will Reuben be alright at the party today?"

"Oh, yeah," Ernie said. "He'll stay in the kitchen most of the time." Of course he wouldn't be alone very often. Ernie's family liked to visit Reuben, one or two at a time.

He said goodbye to the twins and Eliza, then checked on his herd one more time. Peppermint still wore his bumblebee costume. Ernie would have to remember to take that off him later today. The alpaca bumped him in the stomach to say hello.

"Hey boys and girls. I hope you behave today. You made lovely beetles, ants, and bumblebees. Grey won't possibly think his books aren't good enough to publish once he sees you all enacting the picnic scene."

They gathered around him, and Ernie spent a moment with each alpaca and sheep. They were a good herd.

REUBEN WATCHED the party from the kitchen doorway while Pudge dozed in a small dog bed next to the refrigerator. Grammy and Gramps's large barn was used for most of their family events. Since it was freezing outside, Rue's birthday party would have to be mostly indoors. The large barn seemed like the easiest place to have it. The small kitchen at the back had become his refuge.

Dean's papa, Min-Jun, sat close to Grey's abuela, Ines. The two held hands and exchanged shy looks and whispered to one another. Grey and Dean kept circling them, wanting to get close to eavesdrop on what the two were talking about, but trying to respect their privacy.

Reuben snorted. "Min-Jun and Ines."

Juan grinned and picked at a platter of fried mac and cheese balls. "They're fucking adorable, aren't they? Ines is all sassy and pushy while Min-Jun is calm and collected. Grey and Dean are freaking out though."

"They'll get over it. When are they giving Grey his gift?" Reuben asked.

"Elijah said they'll wait until the end." Juan dunked a ball in a small bowl of marinara and ate it in one bite.

"Ernie's worried about you."

Juan propped his head on his fist and sprawled against the small table in the corner. "I want something, Reuben. Something impossible."

"Why impossible?"

"It just is."

Reuben frowned. "Then forget about it."

Juan shook his head, scowling. "That's even more impossible."

Reuben shrugged. "Be miserable for the rest of your life then."

"That is absolutely no help." Juan threw a ball at him.

Reuben caught it and tossed it in his mouth, chewing thoughtfully. "Nothing's impossible. Not really."

Juan looked pensive. "Maybe."

Reuben thought about Ernie. A year ago, Reuben had thought a relationship with someone as social as Ernie would be impossible. Now, they were married with two kids and another on the way. He attended parties and family events and hadn't had a panic attack in a few months. "It's possible, Juan. I promise."

Summer's mother, Fawn, smiled at him as she slid past him. "Do you mind if I share your kitchen, boys?"

"No, ma'am," Juan said, grinning. "Reuben's kitchen is the best place at a party. Cheese ball?"

Fawn popped it in her mouth and moaned a little. "You're magnificent, Reuben."

Reuben nodded. He knew Fawn still felt out of place in Hobson Hills and didn't begrudge her a bit of peace and quiet to collect her thoughts. She had even taken to visiting his kitchen at the pub once a week to talk.

The three of them chatted and kept the party stocked with food. Then, an hour later, Reuben held Ernie in his arms in the kitchen doorway. They watched Rue drag a large gift bag to Grey.

Grey smiled. "Need help opening your present, baby boy?"

"No, Daddy. It's for you," Rue said, grinning. His face was covered in chocolate, and he wore a handmade wooden crown decorated with beads.

Grey looked questioningly at Harper.

The alpha shrugged. He held Auggie in his arms, swaying back and forth. "Don't ask me."

"We love you, Daddy," Rue said. "All of us does. We believe in you."

Grey looked around the room. "What is he talking about?"

Elijah came to stand beside him and helped Rue hold the bag up. Grey's friends and family gathered around. "We all know Melinda wants to publish your books, Grey."

"They're so good," Olive said, bouncing beside her dad. "You can't keep them hidden."

Grey shook his head and pulled the first album from the bag. "What did you guys do?" He flipped through the pages and started laughing. "Oh, god. Jake is the grumpiest mermaid I've ever seen."

"That's what I said," Jules called out from the cake table. "It could be your next book."

"Is that Jimmy and his college friends?" Grey laughed harder. "You guys did this?"

"Look at all of them," David said from Sawyer's lap. "Rue said it, sweet cheeks. We all believe in you."

Grey looked through Elijah and Carter's album. "Aww, Coop and Connor are the friendliest enemies I've ever seen."

"I tried to make them behave," Olive said, shaking her head.

He picked up David and Sawyer's album. "Chunky the bunny rabbit. Wait. Why is Penelope chewing on his tail?"

David shrugged. "She's Sawyer's daughter when she does that."

"She was a cannibal rabbit," Harry said, eyes wide. "Dad didn't feed us in time. We're lucky we escaped with our lives."

Grey laughed. "You poor rabbits."

"Ours next," Linc said, bouncing beside Grey. "I was a really good chef 'till Hucky stole my hat."

Grey laughed. "Summer, you're such a cute raccoon."

The teenager blushed and covered her girlfriend's eyes. "Don't look, Hannah."

Hannah laughed. "Oh, no. This I have to see." She looked over Grey's shoulder. "Aww, you *are* the cutest raccoon ever."

He looked through Bennett and Marco's album next and clapped. "Tomás, you were made to be a troll king. Oh, all of you look great. I can't believe you did all of this." Justin passed his over next, and Grey started crying as he looked through it. "Everyone at The Irish Rose did this for me?"

"We love your books, Grey," Laura called out. "My daughter won't go to sleep until I read one every night."

"Abel and Ernie, you guys too?" Grey wiped his eyes and laughed as he flipped through first Abel's and then Ernie's gifts.

"Look at ours, Daddy," Rue said, bouncing in place as he held out another photo album.

Grey took it and laughed as he flipped through the pictures. "Poor Tiny and Chewie! They look miserable."

"They love you, Daddy." Rue kissed his cheek, spreading chocolate across it. "They was happy."

Grammy pulled out more. "We all did one sweetie. Evan and his friends from school did one, and all the single cousins got together and made one too. We love your books, Grey. You need to share them with the world."

Reuben settled his head on top of Ernie's. He knew how Grey felt. It was hard to give a piece of yourself to someone else. He did it every day when he cooked at The Irish Rose.

"You all are... You all are the best family in the world. Okay," Grey said, wiping his eyes. "I'll do it, guys. I'll send my books to Melinda."

Reuben's eyes met Juan's and he nodded. Taking a risk was frightening, but not taking one was far worse.

OTHER M/M ROMANCE BOOKS BY C.W. GRAY

The Blue Solace Series – science fiction/fantasy, mpreg

1. The Mercenary's Mate – https://amzn.to/2MAOFEH
2. The General's Mate – https://amzn.to/2G1abRE
3. The Soldier's Mate – https://amzn.to/2S7R6ng
4. The Lieutenant's Mate – https://amzn.to/2THZ47w
5. The Engineer's Mate – https://amzn.to/2HpI4vH
6. The Captain's Mate – https://amzn.to/2knP03W
7. The Rebel's Mate – *Coming Soon*
8. Fire's Mate – *Coming Soon*

The Hobson Hills Omegas – non-shifter, mpreg, omegaverse

1. Falling for the Omega – https://amzn.to/2BgWURV
2. Snow Kisses for My Omega – https://amzn.to/2TdDiol

3. Romancing the Omega – https://amzn.to/2UNENKD
4. Healing the Omega – https://amzn.to/2FNcXrY
5. A Pint for my Omega – https://amzn.to/2XItQf7
6. Unraveling the Omega – https://amzn.to/2xRCnRL
7. The Alpha's Christmas Wish – *Coming December 2019*

Hobson Hills Shorts – short stories from the world of Hobson Hills Omegas

1. The Beta's Love Song – https://amzn.to/2UrRPNN
2. Bennett's Dream – https://amzn.to/2GwSpG3
3. Justin's Journey – https://amzn.to/2DhW1t1
4. Grey's Gift – Included in this anthology

The Silver Isles – urban fantasy/paranormal, mermen, mpreg

1. The Guppy Prince – *Coming Soon*
2. The Not so Little Merman – *Coming Soon*
3. The Sea Witch – *Coming Soon*

If you would like to keep up with releases, please like and follow me on Instagram (@c.w._gray) or Facebook (@cwgrayauthor), join C.W. Gray's Reading Nook on Facebook, or visit my website at https://cwgray-author.com.